MIRACLE
SERIES 1

# BEYOND

## AMBER VAN LINGE

A MIGHTY RUSHING WIND
*Publishing*

## BEYOND
**By Amber Van Linge**

First Printing December 2020
Printed in the USA

ISBN: 978-0-578-80465-1

Editing by Laura McIntosh
Cover Design & Book Layout by Jonathan McGraw

Published by A Mighty Rushing Wind Publishing

**www.ambervanlinge.com**

"Don't yield to fear.
All you need to do is
keep on believing."

**MARK 5:36**
*The Passion Translation*

# CONTENTS

# BEYOND

## Chapter One

A miracle is defined as "a surprising and welcome event that is not explicable by natural or scientific laws and is therefore considered to be the work of a divine agency. A highly improbable or extraordinary event, development, or accomplishment that brings very welcome consequences." (dictionary.com)

When people talk about miracles, they speak with a wonder and awe about the event that took place. At times I think we all need to experience a miracle to remind us that there are much greater happenings on the earth than what is going on in the small portion of the world around us. These miracles, when they occur, are so precious they can define a lifetime . . . change the course of a life . . . color a memory . . . mark on our hearts something so unique that they are shared from generation to generation.

Miracles. Miracles are all around us, happening all the time. I think we are usually too busy to see them. We become so used to the miracles in our everyday lives that we lose our wonder. Babies are born. Seasons change. Children grow. If we're not careful we will miss out on the miracle of living life. My name is Grace, and this is where my story begins.

I live in the town of Beyond, Idaho. My family moved to this small, northwestern town when I was two, so the memories of where I was born in California are dim at most. The memories I do have are from stories my dad and mom have told me.

My dad and mom moved our family to Beyond for a new job for my dad and for what Mom said was "a better life balance" for our family. My dad works for Beyond Medical Hospital as an emergency room doctor. He helps people when they need it most.

This is my dad's first job out of residency. It is the kind of job that has no business hours. Dad is always on call, available to talk or make home visits when not on shift at the hospital. Dad has a desire to serve people. He doesn't care whether or not they are able to pay him. Some in Beyond cannot afford to pay for traditional healthcare, so he often comes home with other forms of payment--baked goods, vegetables, fruit, meat, and pretty much anything else imaginable that is made at home. The strangest token he ever brought home was a crocheted turtle with a rock inside to help the turtle hold its shape.

The turtle's head and body was a wonderful shade of green and had a cream-colored underbelly. It had black beads for eyes and pink felt inside its mouth for a tongue. The rock could be slipped in and out of the fabric through a slit on its underside. Mom was unsure what it was to be used for, but I took it straight to my room and found many uses for it.

I named him Timmy the turtle, TT for short. TT became the pet for many of my stuffed animals. My dolls were able to have grand adventures with TT. TT slept at the foot of my bed and held my door open. He liked to hide under my bed when it was unmade, in my closet when I was trying to clean my room, and on my desk when I studied. Timmy was pretty much the best pet ever. Quiet. Never in need of being fed or let out to use the bathroom. Hairless. Never stinky, and I could have him because I wasn't allergic to yarn.

The lady who made TT was so thrilled when she heard I had taken such a liking to her crocheted turtle that she made friends for TT, like Pinky the pig, Doris the dog, and Casper the cat. They all sat one next to the other along my wall at the foot of my bed. I put them there so when I'm in bed I have just to raise my head ever so slightly to see them all sitting there smiling back at me.

Dad and Mom met in their first year of college. As corny as it sounds, they've both said that from the first time their eyes met, they knew they'd be together. Despite their parents' insistence on waiting to marry, they eloped the same year they met. Not long after they eloped, Mom got pregnant with me. They were surprised for sure, but happy nonetheless. I was born November 8 as Grace Avery Sinclair.

Beyond is the type of town that made its name from hosting tourists eager to get out of their busy and frantic lives for a few days of vacation in the outdoors of Idaho. They'd come and take pictures of the beautiful landscapes, hike its majestic mountains, and swim and boat in its large lakes. Beyond is exactly what people expect it to be--a quaint, sleepy town in the fall, winter, and spring but bustling and busy in the summer. Every summer, the population of Beyond swells to almost double its size. I love to walk along the streets when they are full of people and look at all the out-of-state license plates from places I have not yet been able to visit.

Beyond is a place where people receive a friendly "Hello" everywhere they go.

Strangers and visitors often remark, "You never feel like a stranger in the town of Beyond." Boys hold doors for their mamas and remember their pleases and thank yous. Children are safe to walk around by themselves, as neighbors are careful to watch out for one another. Each house in downtown Beyond's tree-lined streets has its own personality, design, and color. It is as if each home has taken on the distinct characteristics of its owner. Some short and wide. Others tall and colorful. Some spacious and grand. Some new, some old. Some run down, while others restored to their original beauty.

Our home, which sits a few streets up from Main Street, is on a large lot with an old maple tree in the front yard. In the fall, the maple tree changes colors from green to yellow, orange, and then brown. It is beautiful. We have lots of grass to play on in our front yard. The small backyard is full of flowers and rows of vegetables that my mom has carefully planted and tended. Our home, sitting well off our street, is a craftsman-style home, white with green and yellow trim. Its wide, wraparound porch is my favorite place during the summer. I enjoy watching the people go by while I sit on one of the many assorted chairs mom has collected over the years.

Our home was built in 1927 and is 80 years older than I am. It has three bedrooms upstairs, one of which is mine. I chose to move into this room after we discovered a small set of stairs hidden inside one of the walls leading to the attic. I just had to have this space as my room, and my parents agreed. I use the space in the attic to create art without giving mom fits about the messes I make. She can't see it, and I'm able to be as messy with my creativity as I desire.

Upon entering our home, large, overstuffed chairs and comfortable couches fill the room that leads to the kitchen from the front door. The kitchen and the basement stairs are towards the back of the house. I like many features about this old home, like the smell of the mothballs in the attic in my room and the way the wood floors squeak when it rains. The house is small, but Mom has made it feel like home.

We've lived here since we moved to Beyond, so it's the only home I know. Creativity lives here. Love lives here. Joy and laughter live here. Faith lives here. Struggle lives here. Fear lives here. Miracles live here.

# MOM
## Chapter Two

Mom's shoulder-length, brown hair becomes wavy when the weather changes. Her wide, blue eyes sparkle like mine when she smiles. Pale skin accentuates the red hue of her lips. She is funny, and when she laughs, the lines around her eyes deepen. I think it makes her look beautiful.

She is the kind of person who walks into a room and brings joy with her. The joy inside her lights up any room. She has learned to find joy, for her life has not always been full of joy.

Mom was raised in a small farming town outside of Bakersfield, California. Her parents, my Grandpa Joe and Grandma Rainey, had two children--the eldest, a boy named David, and my mom Eve.

David was three years older than Mom. By the time David reached high school, he was tall like his dad, handsome, and full of life. He had a strong and adventurous spirit and excelled at everything he did.

To say he couldn't do something was just the challenge he needed to push forward and accomplish it. People loved to be around him. His zeal for life was contagious.

David loved sports. He lettered in every sport he played and was the star of everything he tried. He made it look effortless. He was the point guard on the high school basketball team. His basketball team played well together because David brought out the best in each player.

Mom told me about one of David's basketball games wherein his team ran up and down the court scoring every shot they took. The opposing team was unable to stop any pursuit to the basket they tried to make. David's team made score after score against their opponent. It was a miracle in their midst. No one at the high school before and no team after had ever accomplished what they did that night. At the end of the game, David had scored the most points in the high school's history. The team could not lose with David on their side.

David was the type of brother every sibling wants, the kind in one of those made-for-tv movies. My mom recalls the times they spent talking together in the plum groves surrounding their house. They would lay in the grass dreaming of their futures and calling out the shapes they saw in the clouds. They spent hours together as the dark purple leaves of the plum trees waved in the warm summer breeze.

Their plum farm had been in the family for two generations, beginning with my mom's late grandfather who immigrated to the

United States from Europe in the mid-1900s. When he passed away, he handed the farm down to his son, my mom's papa. David would be the next generation of plum farmers for my family, but I'm not sure what David's thoughts and plans were for his future. It had never been a secret that Papa's desire for him was to be amongst the next generation of plum farmers.

Plum farming is seasonal in central California. The time of sowing new trees, watering, and fertilizing is all in preparation for the midsummer harvest. Mom knew the expectations after school broke for the summer, and on the last day of eighth grade, she prepared her mind as she walked home from the bus stop. She knew, like the summers of the past, she was to help the family pull in the harvest.

The next morning, the first day of summer came early as Mom heard her father's feet moving around on the hardwood floor in the kitchen as he prepared his coffee before heading out to do his morning chores. This was a sound she knew well, her daily wake up call. It was followed by the smell of coffee. During the summer, the light crept through the window early. The shadows of a new day danced over her eyelids, not allowing sleep to continue. As her eyes fluttered open, her mind wandered. She wondered what adventure this new day held.

She rolled out of bed, her hair matted and curled around her face from sleep. As her feet hit the floor, her body started to wake. She sat on the side of the bed while her mind started to orient for the day ahead of her. As she stood up and pulled on the clothes that she had left at the end of her bed, she started to think about all that the day would bring . . . but first, chores.

She headed to the mudroom, just beyond the kitchen. This room had bins for shoes and hooks on the wall to hang jackets and scarves. The bins were organized in order of age, with her father's the closest to the door. Mom found her bin and pulled on her outside boots. David came in next to her as she headed for the door, bumped her out onto the porch and mumbled, "Good morning." David was not a morning person.

Mom had chores to do every morning, every day of the year, rain or shine, school or summer. Her job was to feed the chickens, clean the chicken coop, collect the eggs, and feed the dogs, pick up after them, and then release them for the day.

David, like Mom, had chores that needed to be done first thing in the morning. It may sound oppressive or old world, the workings of farm life, but it was the only life they knew. They had been getting up and working alongside their father for as long as Mom could remember, then when they were old enough, they were given their own chores.

So much needed to be tended to on the farm. David and Mom often worked together to get their chores done more quickly. David cleaned the horse stalls, while Mom groomed and then fed the horses. Then they moved to the pigs. Mom raked the pens, while David rinsed the pigs and threw out day-old scraps for their breakfast. Nothing went to waste. Even the waste was used to help feed the animals or fertilize the garden.

The chicken coop was next. David helped Mom collect the eggs in the cartons that their mom provided. Then they raked the yard and threw out food for the chickens to eat. Mom's favorite part of morning chores was feeding the dogs.

They had two dogs. Both were yellow Labrador retrievers. One was a female named Flower, and the other was a male named Dierks. Papa and Grandma let them choose the names of their dogs. David named the male dog after one of his favorite country singers--Dierks Bentley. Mom named the female Flower on account that when they got her as a puppy during springtime, one of Flower's favorite pastimes was to go from flower to flower, smelling each one as it sprung out of the earth. She smelled the flowers right before rolling around in them. Mom thought she enjoyed the aroma of the flowers so much that she decided she wanted to smell like them. She rolled back and forth, back and forth, with such joy that it made Mom wonder if she should try it as well.

When all of the morning chores were done, David and Mom went back into the house, left their boots in the bins by the door, and handed the freshly collected eggs to Grandma. The smell of bacon filled the air. It popped and jumped on the cast iron skillet waiting to be served. Papa was right behind them. They could hear his stomach growling as they sat down together for the breakfast Grandma had prepared for them. They held hands, and Papa said grace over the food. They started digging into the bowls of scrambled eggs, hash browns, and plates of blueberry muffins and bacon.

Large glasses of milk waited at their places for David and Mom to drink with their meals. The cream on the top of the milk left a mustache on David's upper lip. Mom laughed, and he smiled at her as he wiped it away.

Papa and Grandma made small talk about the day and its plans while David and Mom listened, adding to the conversation during the appropriate breaks. They found out that later that day, a delivery of boxes was scheduled to arrive from a large, regional grocery store chain that purchased the plums the farm produced every year. With the harvest just weeks away, much preparation was happening around the farm with excitement for a good harvest that year.

The beetles that had eaten and destroyed trees and fruit in seasons past, devastating some of their neighbors' crops, were controllable that year. The whole area was excited for the harvest and what the extra finances were going to be able to purchase. The McDouglas' farm was hoping to invest in some new equipment, the Smiths were hoping to put a new roof on their home, and Papa was hoping to make some repairs to the barn and a few other outbuildings.

Every season was a walk of faith. The farmers never knew if the year's crop would be seen through to the harvest. They could control how they tilled, planted, fed, and watered the crops, but so much was uncontrollable. So when the harvest was good, it was a reason to celebrate.

As David and Mom were cleaning up the breakfast dishes, they could see dust wafting in the distance, as a vehicle was coming down the dirt road. Putting his coffee down, Papa rose from the table to greet his guest, calling David to come and join him. David gave Mom a small smile as he threw the dishtowel her way. She sighed as she continued to scrub remains from the pots, pans, and dishes used to cook and serve their breakfast.

When the breakfast dishes were complete, Mom ran out to join her father and David. She watched as they finished unloading the cartons into the barn that held the conveyor belt used for processing all of the plums they harvested. The white and brown cartons had a purple plum stamped onto the side of them. Each carton unloaded was stacked, just sitting and waiting to fulfill its purpose.

Many preparations were made before the harvest. Papa and David checked that the machines were in good working order. They looked over the tree-shaking machine carefully. They went over each part of the motor and mechanical arms, working each part. They tightened, lubricated, and adjusted each area of the machine so it worked as it should. They moved onto the conveyor belt that collected the plums and moved them into large bins. They replaced rollers, removed rusted parts, and carefully examined the conveyor belt. As they were moving through each part, they were bantering back and forth about the latest sports scores, the weather, politics, and the task at hand.

By the end of the weekend, they had checked every part of every piece of equipment to be used to shake, harvest, move, and process the plums. While Papa worked most Mondays, that particular week, he rested in preparation of the weeks ahead that they would be working to collect the harvest.

When harvest day arrived, the family could feel a buzz around the farm as they hurried through an early breakfast to get out at first light. Papa had hired three local men to help with the harvest that year, and everyone was assigned a job.

Papa ran the tree shaker. David helped guide the metal hands that shook the trees. After every three trees, David added lubrication to the metal hands so it didn't damage the trunks of the trees. The first man Papa had hired helped by picking up plums that had fallen in transport from the metal shaking hands to the conveyor belt. The second man and Mom helped remove sticks, leaves, and any other debris from the conveyor belt as they took the plums up to place them in the bin. The third man moved the conveyor belt and bin from tree to tree in alignment with Papa moving the tree shaker.

It was a laborious process. Thousands of trees needed to be shaken over many acres. It took weeks to move through the eight acres of trees ready for harvest. Ladders were used to help harvest the plums that remained in the trees after the machines went through and shook the trees. Each piece of fruit had to be twisted off its branch and placed in a shoot that led below to the waiting bin.

This process could be monotonous. David and Mom tried to make it more fun by having a competition to see who could get the most plums picked the fastest. This was not a competition that Mom usually won, but it was one of the few games they played that helped take their minds off the work.

Most of the fruit remaining on the trees was near the top. David and Mom used tall, A-frame ladders to reach the high-hanging fruit. As they moved around the trees, they adjusted the ladders appropriately. The ground was uneven in many places, which made the legs of the ladders rock back and forth as the weight of their bodies caused the ladders to sway side to side in motion with their momentum as they leaned in and out, in and out to reach the plums.

The competition David and Mom had going caused the swaying side to side to become a rhythm. Somewhere in the back of Mom's mind, she heard her father's voice reminding her to "Stay sharp and mindful in your work, for it is when you start relaxing that accidents can happen."

Back and forth, back and forth. Mom leaned in, twisted, picked, and placed in the shoot. The shoot gently took the fruit into the waiting bin. She started humming as she settled into the rhythm of the movements. She leaned in and twisted the ripe fruit from its branch. Then she leaned back and dropped it on the top of the shoot. The fruit made a soft thud as it landed on top of the other plums that had been picked. The plums they collected now were the fruit they kept and shared.

Grandma made jams and preserves, cakes and tortes, cobblers and crisps. She made them savory. She made them sweet. She canned them, froze them, and dried them. She even made gift baskets with them. If there was a way to use a plum, Grandma knew it.

Towards the end of the harvest day, David and Mom were helping remove the remaining plums from the trees that the shaker didn't drop so Papa could give them away to their neighbors. One way that each farm supported one another was by sharing the harvest with others. Mom was daydreaming about all of her favorite treats her mom would make from the plums they picked, when she heard a scream and a crash. The noise came from the direction she knew David had been picking plums, just a few rows over from her. Quickly she climbed down from her ladder and ran toward the sound.

Back in the house, Grandma was washing dishes. The kitchen windows were open wide when she, too, heard the scream and crash. Quickly turning off the water, she dried her hands and ran through the kitchen door toward the sound.

Both Grandma and Mom ran toward the same sound. Neither of them were sure of what they would find. Mom arrived first. As she approached David, her stomach twisted. David's lifeless body was laying on the ground, a trickle of blood running from his nose. Mom started screaming. Grandma found her cradling David's head in her arms.

Grandma tried to unwind Mom's hands from his head so she could get a better look, but everything in her shouted to hang onto him. Space and time were forgotten. All she could think about was that single drop of red blood trickling from David's nose, running along his upper lip and down his chin.

As Papa approached the place where Grandma, David, and Mom were, his strides got longer. Grandma yelled for Papa to get the car. Papa nodded as he gently persuaded Mom to release her grip on

David's head. He scooped David up as if he were as light as a feather and started running towards his truck.

Grandma and Mom ran after Papa, watching David's head, legs, and arms jostle up and down as Papa ran. When he got to his truck, he effortlessly opened the passenger side door and gently laid David inside. Without a word, he rushed over to the driver's side door and sped away.

Grandma and Mom followed them in the car, silence between them. Neither of them comprehended what they had just seen. Neither of them wanted to understand what they may find when they arrived at the hospital. Mom found herself saying a silent prayer begging God to save her brother, while Grandma drove them closer to David.

After what seemed like an eternity, they arrived at the hospital. As Grandma and Mom rushed in, Ann, the receptionist and one of Grandma's childhood friends, pointed them over to the right. Mom looked down a long hallway with painted white walls and brown wooden doors. Next to each wooden door was a plastic chart holder. They rushed down the hallway, looking into rooms with open doors until they saw Papa near one towards the end. Papa's shoulders were bobbing up and down as he was holding David's hand. All of the machines around the bed were off, and the only sound was Papa's quiet sobs.

Papa looked up and locked eyes with Grandma and Mom. He gently shook his head from side to side. Grandma collapsed to the floor, guttural sounds Mom had never heard from a person coming from her mouth. Mom looked back and forth between her parents' faces, not fully understanding.

Wave after wave of emotion ran through Mom's body until she could no longer hold it all inside of her. She turned on her heel and ran out of the hospital room, past Ann, and out of the building into the blinding sun. She found a bench and collapsed. Having no control over her body, she felt as if she were in a daze. The sounds coming from her mouth were unfamiliar. Void was blossoming in her heart.

The loss of David hung like a dark cloud over Mom's family. The day they buried David was overcast. Even the sun was mourning on that day. So many people came to the house to pay their respects. David's passing sent shockwaves through the farming community. There wasn't a person who didn't know him.

Over the next weeks and months, they found a new cadence as a family. So much of their lives had included David. The void of life without David was painful. Mom found herself staring into his room expecting his presence to still be there and to hear his voice. She imagined she still saw him in so many familiar places. Life, in so many ways, had lost its joy.

Years passed. The feeling of losing David had lost its sting, but everywhere Mom looked in her parents' home, time had stood still. Nothing had been moved, nothing changed. In some ways, she found it strangely comforting.

Papa soon allowed other farmers to work the plum farm. His heart had not been the same since David passed. Over the next several years, he had numerous issues with his body, culminating in a heart attack. Allowing others to farm the land gave them the income they needed to live without putting any more physical stress on Papa's body. People suggested they sell the farm, but Papa wouldn't hear of it.

During Mom's senior year in high school, she was accepted to a university just a few hours north of the farm. She couldn't wait to leave all the memories of David and the home that stood still. Although her parents never voiced their thoughts to her, Mom thought they were thankful for the distraction of her moving. She was the first of her family to attend college, something her mom had wanted for her for as long as she could remember. She felt a new excitement in the house. Change was in the air.

By the time Mom got to college, Papa and Grandma had decided to sell the farm to the man who had been farming their plums. They decided to move into town, telling Mom they wanted to be closer to friends and papa's doctor. Mom was shocked, but she knew they couldn't continue to live suspended in time. She liked to think David was with each of them as they continued to grow older and move on in different ways.

Over summer break between Mom's freshman and sophomore year, Papa passed away, and just two years after that for no apparent medical reason, Grandma passed away as well. Mom was alone, just getting ready to graduate from college. No family, just the memories.

# DAD

## Chapter Three

Dad was raised in a suburb of San Jose, California, called Emerald Hills. This beautiful city made up of farming communities got its name from the grass-covered hills that look like green velvet when the sun shines on them.

His dad worked in San Jose, while his mom stayed home to raise the three children. He has two older siblings. His sister Hannah is four years older than Dad. She is a free spirit who loves animals and people. She always came up with creative ideas, which then would turn into grand adventures for all of the siblings. Steven, his brother, is two years older. Steven is quiet, and growing up, he mostly kept to himself, preferring to build things with his dad's small array of tools than to play with the neighborhood children. Give him a project in which he can use his hands, and he's always willing to help.

Dad was raised on a street where the homes were built on large acres of land and where all the neighbors knew each other. My grandparents had a garden, chickens, an occasional cow, and Trixie the pony. Trixie belonged to Hannah. She was six years old when her parents surprised her with Trixie.

Trixie came from a neighbor whose daughter wasn't interested in having a pony any longer. My grandparents were elated they were able to get Trixie for free, but that was the end of their excitement.

Trixie was a temperamental pony who only liked Hannah because she spent the most time with her. She bribed her by feeding Trixie her favorite treat--apples. Trixie would allow Hannah to ride on her back all over their property, trotting happily from fence to fence. The little saddle she sat on would sway back and forth in rhythm with Trixie's swaying hips. They would ride from Trixie's pen down to the creek so Trixie could get a drink of water and then walk back to the pen, back and forth, back and forth. They walked back and forth so many times it wore away the grass and created a rut. It became the perfect pathway for them to walk together.

If anyone else tried to get on Trixie besides Hannah, Trixie would do a little shimmy and a shake that was incredibly efficient in getting the rider off her back. When Hannah wasn't around, Dad tried many times to win Trixie's affections, with no success. It was clear Trixie was capable of loving just one person at a time, and that person was Hannah. As Hannah got older, her interests changed, and she eventually lost interest in Trixie. The trail they had blazed together covered again with grass. Trixie seemed happy to spend her days grazing in the field and being left alone to wander around her gated area. Once my grandparents recognized her waning interest in having a pony, they decided to give her away to another little girl, and with that, another young girl's dreams of owning a pony lived on with a new family.

One summer, Hannah had the idea to build a boat to float into town. All the siblings really liked going into town, but they lived three miles outside of town. That equated to a 30 minute bike ride or 45 minute walk. So the thought of a quicker way to get there was exciting!

Everyone would be amazed at how well it would sail down the water, how fast it would go, and at how well it was made. Hannah painted the picture of her vision to my dad and uncle. Their skeptical faces turned from disinterest to great excitement as they started to plan everything needed to build such a boat.

From that day forward, they spent every day down by the creek that ran through their property, building the boat that would take them into the city. Their dad gave them some of the firewood used for the furnace that warmed the house. My dad and uncle then spent at least a dozen hours cutting the wood down to the right size to bind together for the bottom of the boat. My grandma donated fabric from her sewing bin for the sail. Hannah and Dad went on a treasure hunt, searching the garage and outside shed for all of the other materials they needed to complete the boat. They found rope for hoisting the sail and keeping the wood together, nails, hammer, paint, and various other supplies they thought they may need to complete their boat.

They named the boat *Trixie* in honor of Hannah's pony. Hannah painted the picture of a horse on the side of the boat and wrote

*Trixie* on the back. Finally after many weeks of work, the boat was ready! All they had to do was try her out to make sure she could float.

Steven and Hannah pulled, and Dad pushed *Trixie* as hard as they could off the shore into the water. Dad felt the earth give way with each pull that they made. "Pull!" Dad yelled, and they pulled with all of their might, inch by inch until she was in the water! Dad held onto his rope as she floated on the water for the first time. They didn't give a second thought as the three of them jumped aboard and started paddling away from the shore.

Steven raised the sail up from the place it laid on the boat, and they started to pick up some speed. They passed by some of their neighbors' houses until they came near the main road. The water turned them, so they were now sailing parallel to the road.

They experienced a sense of accomplishment, pride, and euphoria at what they had done.

Cars with curious passersby looked towards them with questioning faces. When the siblings later reflected, their questioning faces should've been a warning of what was ahead, for what they didn't know was that this seasonal creek would narrow soon, ending this grand adventure prematurely.

Hannah saw it first and exclaimed, "Uh oh, hey, guys!" Their gazes followed her pointed finger. Ahead of them, the creek narrowed into a sewer pipe. Their boat came to an abrupt stop as it turned into the dam. All the water that rushed them down the creek built up behind their boat. They climbed off onto either side of the creek bank, watching helplessly as their beloved boat was being tossed to and fro into the dam. As they watched, the water forced their boat against the dam over and over again until parts of the boat began to break loose. It didn't take long before the power of the water won the boat over, and piece by piece, *Trixie* surrendered until nothing was left.

After they watched the last of the boat disappear, they silently began the walk back home. The walk to the house seemed like an eternity. How could they have traveled so far so quickly? It seemed to have been just a moment that they were on the boat with joy in their hearts and excitement on their lips. They had traveled over two miles from the house.

As car after car passed them on the road, they trudged along, slowly making their way closer and closer to their house. Out of the corner of Dad's eye, he saw a small blue car pass them. He didn't pay any attention to it until it pulled over in front of them. The curly-haired, blond head of Dad's friend Steve's sister Joan popped out of the driver's side window, and asked, "Hey, can you all use a ride?" Exhaustion had taken over by this point. All of the adrenaline had left their bodies, leaving them with a feeling of exhaustion. With the offer of a ride home, they found a new energy, and they ran and quickly piled into the waiting car.

As Joan pulled back onto the road, they recounted the whole story again. She thought they were crazy and said so. She asked them what their next adventure was going to be, and that got the three of

31

them thinking and planning again. Even Joan got into it. They made suggestions for a hot air balloon adventure, a derby car, or maybe even a safari. By the time they got home, they were all laughing. Most of the disappointment of their boating failure had disappeared. They were moving on to their next adventure having greatly enjoyed the last one. What they didn't know in those waning moments in the car with Joan was that this would be their last adventure together.

The next day, Grandpa and Grandma went into town, leaving the three children at home to start planning for their next adventure. This was a day not unlike most others. The temperature was warm, but a nice breeze blew into the house through the open windows.

Grandpa and Grandma occasionally went into town together. Grandpa went in daily during the work week for his job while Grandma usually stayed with the children. As they ate breakfast together as a family that morning, there was an underlying feeling of tension that at the time Dad felt but didn't recognize. Both of his parents were trying just a little too hard to normalize the breakfast activity. Grandma pushed the food around on her plate, making small talk about the previous day's adventure. She asked questions she already knew the answers to, and Grandpa was quiet, making the occasional responsive sound to the conversation.

Finally breakfast was over, and the three children were tasked with helping clean up the kitchen as their mom and dad prepared to leave together. Grandma came in and kissed each one goodbye, with Dad being last. She whispered in his ear as she kissed his cheek, "I love you more than you will ever know." As she spoke, Dad heard

Grandpa calling to her that it was time to go. She walked toward the door, pausing as she reached it to look back at her children working together to finish cleaning the kitchen. She sighed and quietly closed the door behind her.

That was the last time they had breakfast in their home as a family. The appointment Grandpa and Grandma had together was with an oncologist--a cancer doctor. Grandma had been experiencing some abdominal pain for a while. A few weeks before, she had gone to see their family doctor. The family doctor ran a few tests to try and diagnose the source and cause of Grandma's pain. The blood test came back with an unusual increase of white blood cells. As a result, the doctor ordered an abdominal CT scan. A few days later, they found out it was cancer.

My grandparents decided not to tell their children until they knew more about the prognosis. That day at the oncologist didn't bring hope. The outlook was not good, as the cancer was in her pancreas. The doctor gently explained that Grandma had three or so months to live and walked through some treatment options that could, with no guarantees, extend her life for an unknown amount of time. One thing was certain to both of them as they stared at the doctor trying to digest what he was saying--life was never going to be the same.

When they came home that day, they walked through the door hand in hand, eyes puffy. My dad had never before seen his dad cry. They called all three of the children over to the couch and told them the news. Pancreatic cancer was all Dad heard. As they spoke, he watched Steven's mouth drop open and then form a thin, tight line on his face as his dad continued to talk. When Hannah began to cry, their mom moved over to comfort her. They all were in shock. There were tears and many questions that were impossible to answer. Grandpa and Grandma did their best to answer questions and provide comfort. Unaware of what was to come, fear set in Dad's heart.

Over the proceeding few weeks, Grandma had more doctor's appointments. The cancer in her pancreas was also in some of the surrounding tissues. These findings caused complications. She started chemotherapy and radiation. With Grandpa having to work and none of the kids being old enough to drive, their home became a hive of activity. People from the church, neighborhood, and community seemed to be at the house every waking hour. People from the church helped feed the family by bringing meals. Friends from the neighborhood picked Grandma up for her appointments or treatments and then dropped her back off at the house when they were done. Various people from the community came by to cut the grass, pull weeds, and tend to the inside house cleaning. My dad had never seen such an outpouring of people willing to help.

For the children, it was a great distraction. For Grandpa, it was a great help. For Grandma, it was a relief, especially as her health began to decline. The chemotherapy and the radiation took their toll on her body. She had always been full of energy and life, but most days now she was late getting up in the morning. When she did get up, she'd complete a few tasks and then need to lay down again. Everything was much harder for her. The majority of her energy went towards trying to heal her body. Cancer stole her hair, her appetite, and her body. Grandma became a shell of who she had been.

Two months after Grandma had been diagnosed with cancer, she began to experience some back pain. Pain was not new to her in this treatment process, so she hadn't thought much about it. Her doctor decided to run a few tests. The results were not good. The doctor told her the cancer in her pancreas was not responding to the treatments. The test also found a new growth near her spine, which explained her back pain. Her doctor gave her some new treatment options, but my grandparents decided it was time to stop the treatments and to live in the fullness she was able to for the rest of the time she had.

Grandma had good days and bad days after she quit treatment. Some days she seemed stronger, but on others she seemed weaker. One of my dad's favorite things to do with his mom on the days she was not feeling well was to sit in bed with her, resting his head on her shoulder and snuggling into the pillows with her while she read. It didn't really matter what she was reading. Dad just wanted to be close to her. He sat with his eyes closed for as long as her energy held out and imagined the words she painted with each rise and fall of her voice.

On Grandma's good days, the family visited all of their favorite local places, making new memories and recalling old ones. Funny times and sad times . . . each memory was precious. Each one was a seed planted in their hearts. Each of them were unknowingly being released in new directions and passions because of what was happening to their mom. The memories of those days were good. They would be the ones they'd keep with them forever.

Weeks turned into months. Grandma got to a point of being in so much pain that the doctor suggested she be admitted to the hospital until her pain was manageable at home again. Her family visited her almost every day that they could. The nurses and doctors were kind.

One doctor who oversaw Grandma's care had caramel candies in his pocket. When he came to see her, he gave my dad and his siblings each a caramel candy. The candy was a welcome treat and distraction from the questions he was asking their mom. The doctor had a kind smile and was soft spoken. In Dad's young mind, the doctor was like a superhero coming in to help his mom. Every time he came in, the atmosphere in the room changed. He couldn't put his finger on it at the time, but there was something different about him.

He was not different in a bad or weird way but different in a calming, peaceful way. He brought good news or somber news daily. One would think that when he walked in, everyone would feel apprehension at the news he was going to bring, but all Dad felt was an overwhelming sense of care. When matched to the tone and the kind words he spoke, it brought peace into the room that lingered even after he departed.

One day after school, Dad was sitting on his mom's hospital bed, telling her about his day. The doctor he liked came in to speak to his mom. The same peace that Dad had felt time and time again returned, but that day, it didn't last. The doctor's face was long and somber that time. It was not good news. Her body was shutting down, and they could do nothing more for her except help her to continue to manage the pain. Grandma looked at him, took his hand, and remarked, "It is as I expected it to be. You've been kind with me and my family. Would it be okay for me to go home now?"

The doctor smiled at her and replied, "I'll have the nurses start preparing the discharge paperwork. We will send people to come and help with your care at home. It has been my greatest pleasure to oversee your care. I know I will see you again." His eyes twinkled as he said those last words, words that would resonate in my dad's heart as they prepared to bring his mom home.

Just a few days after they brought her home, Grandpa called all his children into their bedroom. Noisy machines surrounded their mom, each one making a different sound. As they entered that morning, the machines had all been turned off, and the only noise was coming from their mom--a shallow, inconsistent breathing sound. Grandma's night nurse was nowhere to be seen. It was just Grandpa, Grandma, and their children. As they entered the room, their dad looked up at them. He said the words they knew were coming but were hard to comprehend. "It's time." They all sat huddled around the bed as their mom peacefully took her last breaths. There were many tears. Steven ran from the room, the stillness of the silence suffocating.

The days that followed were a blur. Grandpa made the arrangements for the funeral just the way his wife desired. It was a beautiful celebration of her life, and most of the town came out to her funeral. The wake to follow was held at the house with lots of food and shared memories about Grandma. After everyone had left and the last bits of food cleaned up, the four family members sat around in the living room together. No words were said, each one processing the day in their own way.

They laid her to rest the next day. The pastor who was at the gravesite spoke about heaven--a place where she was no longer in pain, no longer suffering. Many nice people said kind words about her, but it didn't change the fact that Dad missed her terribly. There was a mom-shaped void in him.

In the days and months after she died, the mom-shaped void looked different in each one of them. Grandpa didn't say much those days. He came home from work, found his chair, and sat and drank until it was time to go to bed. Most nights he passed out and ended up sleeping in his recliner. Dad thought that losing his wife broke his dad's heart. His children were a constant reminder of her, of happier times. He wanted to numb his feelings. He disengaged from life, alcohol becoming his crutch. Soon, he was unable to work, lost in his sorrow and pain.

After Hannah and Steven graduated high school, they left home. Hannah moved to San Francisco to go to cosmetology school, and Steven joined the military. The house was filled with memories of their mom. My dad became Grandpa's caretaker after Hannah and Steven left. After Dad graduated from high school, he went to the local junior college during the day and came home after work to make sure his dad ate, bathed, and had clean clothes.

A few neighbors helped my dad with Grandpa. They came by the house to visit with him, checking in to make sure he was okay while

Dad was gone. This was working well until Dad got a call at work that brought him to the hospital. One of the neighbors had gone to check on Grandpa and found him unconscious on the floor. He had lost his balance trying to reach for something out of a cabinet, slipped, and hit his head on the counter. No one was sure just how long he had been unconscious. The neighbor called the ambulance and then called my dad.

By the time my dad arrived at the hospital, they had stabilized Grandpa, but he had not regained consciousness. So many tubes and machines were connected to him. As Dad was standing there looking down at him, all the memories of being in the hospital with his mom when she was sick came rushing back. He sobbed, alone, at the foot of the bed.

When he felt a hand on his shoulder, he looked up and saw the kindly face of the doctor who helped his mom. He was so relieved to see a familiar face. He wiped his tears with his sleeve as the doctor handed him a tissue to blow his nose. They made small talk until Dad regained his composure. After he had collected himself, the doctor told him that the machines around his dad were keeping him alive. He pointed to one machine that he said helped regulate the swelling on his brain, then to another that was helping him breathe, and lastly to a tower that automatically dispersed medicine so he was without pain. He said that Grandpa had very little brain activity. He recommended that my dad call the family who wanted to say goodbye.

The realization of what he was saying pushed Dad back to find support in the nearest chair. So many emotions ran through his mind--unbelief, grief, sadness, and relief. The kind eyes of the doctor were compassionate, and Dad felt in that one look that he understood all the emotions he was feeling.

Dad had to concentrate on his numb fingers as he dialed the phone numbers for Hannah and Steven. Steven arrived later that night and stayed in Grandpa's room, sleeping on the opposite side of his bed from Dad. Hannah came early the next morning, breaking Steven and Dad to go grab coffee and breakfast from the hospital cafeteria.

Again, their whole worlds stopped. All of the memories of the last days with their mom came rushing back to them. The three siblings talked about those days as they sat around their dad. They talked about how much had changed in the years since their mom had died. As they sat around their dad sharing memories (the good, bad, and funny ones), Steven looked over at his dad's face. He was smiling. Somewhere in my dad's heart, he believed that Grandpa could hear them, and that was what made him smile.

The kindly doctor came in again to talk with them. He explained that Grandpa no longer had brain function and gave the options. Dad never thought they would have to make this kind of decision. How could they choose whether someone continues to live or not? As the doctor left the room, Dad looked around at his siblings' faces. He could tell they mirrored the emotions he was feeling. As they talked, they became more resolute to let their dad live. They had already lost one parent. They weren't going to willingly choose to lose another. They told the doctor their decision. He nodded, not in agreement, but it was a nod of confirmation that he had understood their desires.

With that decision, the three of them left the hospital to go and find a restaurant.

As they were finishing dinner, Steven received a call from the hospital that sent them rushing back to the hospital. As they arrived, they found the last of the hospital staff leaving Grandpa's room. During dinner, his breathing had changed. The staff did all they could, but he was ready to go. He had no more fight in him. He had fought for his wife, fought to keep his family together, and fought for his sanity, but in the end, he had nothing left to fight for himself.

They entered the room. It was eerily quiet with no more beeps or the hum of the machines around him helping him breathe and keeping an eye on his vital signs. They had all been turned off, and Grandpa lay there on the bed in the stark white room of the hospital with a small smile on his face. He looked happy, Dad decided. Hannah cried, while Steven and Dad sat on opposite sides of the bed holding his hands. He was still warm as they sat there soaking up the last minutes of being with him.

The hospital staff was kind. They let them stay until they were done saying their goodbyes. Then someone from the hospital morgue came in, covered dad's face, and wheeled him out of the room. As they exited the room, the kindly doctor spoke words that brought great comfort.

He looked at Dad and asked, "How old are you, son?"

Dad replied, "I just turned twenty." He then asked if Dad was in school. He told him he was, explaining to him that he was attending a local junior college, holding down a full-time job, and he had been caring for his dad. The kindly doctor nodded in response. Then he said something to my dad that changed his whole life.

"I saw the way you cared for your dad," he said. "You sacrificed a lot for him. Have you ever thought about becoming a doctor?" The kindly doctor went on to encourage Dad by telling him that he thought he would make a good doctor. He gave him his card and told Dad when he was ready, he would help him find a job in the hospital.

Something happened in him that day as the doctor encouraged him. In the middle of Dad's grief, a new flame of purpose ignited--a hope for his future.

# GRACE

## Chapter Four

I am smallish, with blond, curly hair that bounces when I run. My brown, almond-shaped eyes are a shade darker than creamed coffee, with just a hint of gold that sparkles when I smile. My button nose has a small bump on the bridge, just like my mom's. It isn't a large bump, but when I put my hand to the bridge of my nose, I can feel the perfectly round shape of cartilage just under the skin. My mouth is thin and nicely shaped, and my wide teeth are completely squared. All these features are arranged on a heart-shaped face. Some would say I am cute and others beautiful. I would say I like the way I look.

Yesterday was the last day of sixth grade. Next year, I will go to a new school for junior high. The thought of starting a new school is exciting and terrifying at the same time. For now, I will enjoy the long, sunny, warm summer days.

I am excited for all that summer holds. It's not that I don't like school. Elementary school was filled with friends and fun activities, but the days were monotonous. I crave unlimited time to spend doing the activities I want to do.

As an only child, I have been entertaining myself for as long as I can remember. I have a flair for the dramatic and love being creative. I find the smallest of trinkets that once my imagination takes hold, can keep me occupied for hours. My favorite objects are the miscellaneous items around the house that I can repurpose to make into other creations. I make beautiful designs out of toilet paper cardboard, scraps of paper, plastic spools, yarn, or anything I can find. Almost nothing is trash in my eyes.

I have been keeping tiny plastic spools that were left over from a toy loom I had received as a gift, in a red drawstring bag. Today is the day I will repurpose them. I cut a piece of cardboard from a box my mom had received in the mail. I then glue a colorful piece of paper to the cardboard. While the glue dries, I cut another piece of cardboard from the box. I carefully lay out each spool on the cardboard and set to work painting each spool a different color. As I work, I hum a song of which only I know the words. Before long, all of the plastic spools are painted in bright, cheerful colors. When I am done, my stomach starts growling. As the spools begin drying, I wander downstairs to see what I can find in the pantry to eat.

I find my mom in the kitchen finishing up the dishes. "Mom, I'm hungry. Is there anything to eat?"

Mom exhales noticeably, turning on her heel to face me as she answers, "We just finished eating, Grace."

"I know, but I'm already hungry again."

Mom replies, "That probably means you didn't eat enough, my love." She walks over to give me a hug. "Okay, here are some things you can eat." We talk back and forth as we work side by side putting together a snack. I love working alongside Mom. There is something soothing about her presence. I've always felt it. When she walks into a room, she brings a calm to any situation. It is something both my mom and dad have in common--they are both peacemakers.

Mom asks me what my plan is for the day. I tell her about the project I have going on upstairs. She asks me what I'm going to do with all of the colored spools now that they are painted. I have to think for a moment before responding, "I don't know. I thought I would just glue them onto the colored paper, but maybe there is something more I should be doing with them."

Mom recommends I make designs with them. She looks at me and suggests, "Close your eyes. Picture all of the different colored plastic spools."

"Okay," I reply. "I can see them."

"How should they be arranged?" she asks me.

As she continues to talk, I start seeing shapes. "I see them!" I said with great excitement. I open my eyes and give her a big hug. As I release my mom, I look her in the eye and remark, "Thank you, Mom!"

She releases me to run back to my room with the words, "Always welcome, my love."

How many times in life do we only see the surface value of something? Then someone else comes along and points out something new--something we didn't see before then. Familiarity with the way something is supposed to function doesn't breed creativity, but when someone else can see something we can't, all of a sudden we see with new eyes.

I have such a feeling of anticipation as I run to my room. My mind is full of ideas, new ideas, of shapes and patterns I can put together with my colored spools. I spend the next couple of hours designing, creating, and gluing together the shapes and patterns I see in my mind. As I stand back to admire all of the new masterpieces I had created, mom walks in and stands next to me admiring and commenting on my new creations.

"They are beautiful! My favorite is this red one with the orange, yellow, and gold accents. It almost looks like the fire is alive and racing off of the page!" Grace smiles under her mom's praise. "I'm heading into town to drop Dad's lunch off and do some shopping," Mom explains. "Would you like to come with me?"

I don't have to think long. "Yes!" I exclaim.

One of my favorite places to go is to visit Dad at the hospital. Almost all of my favorite people are there. As we get into the car, I start thinking about the art project I had just finished. Maybe I should've brought some of them with me to share with my friends. As I am contemplating this idea, my mom breaks into my thoughts. "What are you thinking about, Grace?" So I tell her. She pulls to the side of the road and then makes a U-turn.

"What are you doing?" I ask.

Turning around, she replies, "We have time to go back to get your art."

I smile, as my heart skips. "Thank you, Mom!"

I run back into the house, carefully collect all of my projects, grab a pen, and head for the door. As I step back into the waiting car, I thank Mom for coming back to the house. I spend the rest of the drive into town assigning names to the art pieces I created and carefully print the name of whom each one was for in the lower right hand corner.

As we walk into the hospital emergency room lobby, Elizabeth's face brightens. Elizabeth is Beyond Hospital's emergency room admissions coordinator. She has worked for the hospital, as she says, "from the day I was born!" As she grew up, her father was the Beyond Hospital administrator, so she spent most of her youth here. She finds great delight in greeting people as they come into the hospital.

Elizabeth is calm under pressure. She has a joyful countenance and is an all-around happy person. Her brown, curly hair is pulled back today in a loose ponytail. She is a large woman but moves easily for someone her size. She demonstrates that as she quickly comes around the desk to give us a hug. As she greets us, the sound of her voice rings out, echoing off the walls of the emergency waiting room. Eyes turn towards us as she expresses her joy in having us visit her today.

"Just two of my favorite people!" Elizabeth exclaims. We exchange greetings, and her gaze drifts down to my hands. "Well, mercy child! What creation have you brought to us today?" she asks me. I sift through the papers until I find the one I have carefully printed with her name. It is bright and cheerful like her. I hand it to her. She touches my arm, tears coming to her eyes as she thanks me for thinking of her.

The doors to the emergency room open and Ryan, one of the ER's nurses, walks out with tablet in hand, ready to call in the next patient. He looks over at the three of us, smiles, and walks towards us. Ryan is the type of nurse that when he smiles, his entire body radiates. From the small wrinkles around his eyes, to his gentle bedside manner, he is one of my favorite people to see. He is kind, strong, and also a favorite of the patients. He gently hugs me close as he greets Mom and winks at Elizabeth.

I hand him the picture I made for him. It is of a tree, its trunk wide and strong. Its branches extend toward the sky and are filled with bright green leaves. As I was piecing this picture together, I had no one else in mind as I widened the base of the tree trunk and filled in the sky with birds.

As one of the newer staff members to the hospital and to the city of Beyond, Ryan works often with Dad. He has come to our house many times since arriving, as he likes to help Dad with projects around the house. He is sociable and loves to help. He is single, so he has time to devote to helping others when he is not helping others at work. I like to watch them work together. They spend hours doing mundane tasks around the house as they talk. Sometimes I will listen to their conversations. Dad is a good listener, and so am I. I hear pain sometimes in Ryan's voice. I know from what Mom and Dad have said that Ryan has come here to escape from something, although I don't know why he is in Beyond. It doesn't matter much to me.

That is why Ryan's smile is so big when he sees me in the ER lobby. He had given me the loom with the little spools after he had found them at a garage sale. When he saw them, he thought of me and purchased them. He gave them to me over dinner one night. As he slid the loom across the table, I saw my mom and dad's faces smiling at the expression of pure joy that spread on my face. I jumped up, ran around the table, and threw my arms around his neck. I asked to be excused from the table, knowing I wouldn't be able to eat another bite. Mom and Dad allowed me to escape from the table.

My mind wanders back to the present and tries to re-engage into the conversation that is going on around me when I hear the screeching tires of an ambulance pull up outside the building. The automatic doors of the ER swing open as the EMTs bring an emergency case with them. Ryan smiles and hurries over to the doors that lead back to the ER by pushing in a code that swings them open wide. With a wave, he follows the gurney back into the emergency room to begin treating the ER's next emergent patient.

We watch the commotion until the doors to the emergency area close. Saying goodbye to Elizabeth, we head down a hallway to see Dad. Around this time is usually when he is scheduled for a break. We find him a few moments later in the staff break room. He rises as we walk in to greet him. He comes around to kiss Mom and give me a hug. He starts telling us about some of the interesting cases he has seen so far today on his shift, as Mom begins to unpack the lunch we will share together.

Dad works three, twenty-four-hour shifts a week. We come and visit him when he is on shift to bring him food and spend time with him. Today Mom has brought lunch for us all to share. As she unpacks the basket she brought, we talk about my latest art project. Mom and Dad's conversation turns to topics that don't interest me, and my mind wanders as I watch Charlotte, another doctor in hospital, come through the doors of the break room.

Charlotte delivers babies. She is what I would call handsomely pretty. Something about the way she looks is unique. Her square, black glasses are just a bit too big for her face, making her face appear smaller than it actually is. As she approaches our table, the black, square frames slip down on her nose. She stops by our table to exchange pleasantries and then heads to her own table in the corner of the room. Dad says she is stern but good at what she does.

Mom lowers her voice as she walks away from our table to say something for our ears alone. I catch a bit of what she is saying, but a pain that starts pulsating behind my eyes keeps me from hearing what mom is saying. I close my eyes. The pain is sharp and blurs my vision. As quickly as the pain comes, it disappears. I open my eyes, able to focus again on my parents' conversation.

Much too soon, Dad receives a text from the emergency room. He is needed again. He hugs Mom and me and walks out of the room. Mom and I wave goodbye to Charlotte as we follow Dad out of the breakroom. We weave our way back down the hallways to the emergency room's waiting room. Elizabeth is on the phone as we enter. I turn my head to wave goodbye to Elizabeth, and the sharp pain behind my eyes returns. I am momentarily blinded. Then my vision clears, the pain disappears, and I am able to see Elizabeth. I shake my head. This pain is so strange. As quickly as the pain comes, it disappears, and I am able to focus again on the present. Elizabeth waves goodbye to us as she speaks to the person on the other end of the phone.

# THE PAIN
## Chapter Five

Walking out of the hospital to the car I turn to Mom and say, "I have been having these shooting pains in my head." She stops and turns to me with a look of concern on her face.

"How long has this been going on?" I share with her the few times over the past month I have experienced this pain. I tell her how suddenly it comes, and then it just goes away quickly. Shrugging my shoulders, I look up at Mom and see that her eyes are glassy. As I watch her, I can tell that my revelation of what is happening to me is taking her back to a place that is full of pain and emotion.

I take her hand in mine, and ask, "Mom, are you okay?" My touch to her hand seems to draw her back to the present.

She continues, "Do you remember me telling you about my brother David?" I nod my head, vaguely recalling her talking about her brother. It is not something she often discusses. "He was just a little older than you when he died. I do wish you had the opportunity to know him. You would've liked him. The reason I bring him up now is that you talking about your pain takes me back to the last time I saw David. It was in a hospital like the one your dad works at." Her words trail off as she shakes her head and continues.

"I am concerned about the pain you are experiencing, Grace. It is not normal. Would it be okay for us to talk to Dad tonight about your pain and see what he recommends?" she asks.

I had expected this response. Maybe that is why I didn't tell her sooner. I wasn't ready to know why I am experiencing pain. I shrug my shoulders and reply, "Yes, that would be okay."

I don't want to talk about my pain anymore. My revelation seems to have changed the tone for the rest of the errands we needed to do. Clearly Mom's mind is distracted as we go from store to store. I don't like it when Mom worries. I can sense her unease, and I dislike being the cause of it. I can't wait to get home to escape.

When I get home, I do just that--escape upstairs to the attic. I throw myself into the piles of pillows and blankets on the floor and turn my head to look out at our neighbors' home.

I sit up and make my way to my art table that faces the window and begin drawing. The sound of the pencil on the page as it makes its way back and forth on the surface of the page distracts my mind, allowing me to subconsciously focus on something other than my present situation. I don't know how long I sat there, but as I near the end of drawing my picture, Mom calls me down to eat dinner. I look up for the first time in what seems to me to be a long time to see the sun much lower in the sky than I remember it being. I mentally shrug my shoulders and move out of my chair. After being in one position for I don't know how long, my body complains as I stand. Stretching, I make my way downstairs.

As I walk into the dining room, dinner is already on the table. Mom and Dad are in conversation together. Their body language reflects one of intimacy and interest as they speak in quiet voices across the table. I look at the table and then back to them. The table is filled with all my favorite foods. "Yayy!" I exclaim. The fact that all of my favorite foods are prepared and waiting for me probably should've alerted me to something, but I am only focused on my hunger.

They smile at me as I sit down to join them.

Dad asks, "Shall we pray and bless our food?"

I nod and bow my head as he prays over the food. We start to pass the food. Four dishes are on the table--macaroni and cheese, chicken nuggets, cheese pizza, and a good-sized spinach salad. Silence is around the table as we pass the food to one another and fill our plates. I close my eyes as I take the first bite of pizza. My stomach responds with its last hungry cry as my pizza makes its way down to it.

Mom is the first to break the silence.

She starts off by saying, "So, Grace, you were telling me earlier, as we were leaving the hospital, about the pain you've been experiencing. Will you tell your dad about the pain?"

My father puts his fork down as I begin to speak, giving me his undivided attention. This is the way I imagined him looking at the patients he sees in the emergency room, with his hands folded and kindness in his eyes as he intently looks at them, nodding in understanding of the words that are being spoken.

"Well," I say, "it started a few weeks back. I was in my first period class. I had been in a rush that morning and slid into my seat just seconds before the late bell rang. I was thankful to have made it to my seat before the bell rang. As I sat down and my breathing slowed, pain started to make its way up the back of my neck. For a moment the pain was so intense my vision went blurry, and then everything went black. As quickly as the pain came, it disappeared, and everything returned to normal. Honestly, I didn't know what to think," I say as I shrug my shoulders.

I confess to my parents that after the strange pain happened at school that day, I didn't say anything to anyone about the episode until I was walking home after school that afternoon with my best friend Betsy.

Betsy and I have been friends since kindergarten. Most of my earliest memories are with her. Her family is an extension of my family. She has long, mousy blond hair that she wears pulled back from her face. Her bright blue eyes are highlighted by the lightest sprinkling of freckles across her milky white skin.

I've always liked her freckles and the way they run over the bridge of her nose ever so lightly. It reminds me of when Mom and I sprinkle powdered sugar through a sift over our Christmas cookies. We add just enough sugar that provides the perfect amount of sweetness to complete the look of the cookie--the perfect touch. Betsy's freckles are the perfect touch to her face.

My mom likes to tell the story about the first time I met Betsy. I liked her freckles so much that when I came home that day, I took a brown marker and added large brown circles to my nose. I was quite pleased with my new freckles, until Mom came into my room. The look on her face registered surprise. She asked me what I used to make the brown circles. She gasped when I handed her the brown permanent marker. We laugh about it now, but the brown stain from the marker I used on my face stayed for days. No matter how much we rubbed or what we used, the color didn't fade.

Walking home from school that day with Betsy, I started to tell her about my strange experience during class. She looked at me with concern on her face as we walked. She exclaimed, "Wow! That sounds terrible! Has that happened before?" I hesitated before responding because as she was talking, I did remember one other time that this pain had come. It was over a year ago, and it had come and gone quicker than this one, but the pain was the same. I mentioned to her the brief time it had previously happened. The crease in Betsy's brow furrowed deeper. I asked her not to say anything, and despite the look of concern on her face, Betsy nodded her head in agreement.

"Pinkie swear!" I demanded and reached out my pinkie toward Betsy.

Betsy hesitantly reached out her pinkie and said, "Pinkie promise." A pinkie promise was the ultimate promise between friends. I knew now I could trust Betsy not to share my secret.

We walked the rest of the way to her house in silence. Betsy waved goodbye and disappeared through the front door of her house, which was just three doors down from mine. I made the remainder of the short walk to my house quickly.

Unlocking the side door, I entered the garage. I opened the door to the mud room and shrugged out of my jacket, hanging it just inside the door on a hook that has my name above it. As I sat down on the bench below my hook, I pulled off my shoes one by one and put them in a box also with my name on it.

A heaviness came over me, and I leaned back into the wall for support, my head resting on the bottom of my jacket. I was weary-- weary in a way I had never experienced. A tiredness spread across my body. It felt like it had reached all the way down into my bones. Mom wasn't home, so having the house to myself, I slowly walked the short distance up the stairs to my room and flopped face down on my bed.

The next thing I remember, Mom was gently shaking me awake. I rubbed my eyes, and her face came into focus. She had a look of concern on her face as she placed her hand on my head and asked, "Are you feeling okay, Grace?"

I shrugged my shoulders. "I don't feel sick," I commented. "At least I don't think I do." My voice caught as I hesitated, unsure if what I was saying was the truth or not. Either way, I could tell my response had made my mom feel better, for the crease in between her brow went from that deep space that only mothers' faces can make when they are concerned to a more relaxed line between her eyebrows.

"That was the last time I had pain until today," I tell my parents. My mind wanders in and out of the dinner conversation. I make the appropriate head nods and verbal responses as they speak, but my mind is far from the conversation, as I am eager to return to my room.

When dinner is over, I help Mom in the kitchen, but I excuse myself quickly after helping with the dishes by telling her I have something to finish upstairs. All the while, the thoughts in my head pull me back to my room. I can't wait to get on my computer and start searching online for reasons for the pain episode that day.

My mind starts swirling again as I sit down in front of my computer to find something wrong inside of me. My dad has warned me that self diagnosing on the internet is dangerous, as it usually leads to assuming the worst case scenario. The search engine is only as smart as the person who is typing in the words, and it does not have the advantage of imparting discernment with a person or seeing the patient as a whole like a doctor does.

I search for head pain. As I scroll down, I see search results for headaches, stress, and migraines. Eeeek! Wrong word, I think. I know what a headache feels like. The pain I have experienced was sharp and intense. As quickly as it came on, it left. The next result listed is migraines. I click on the hyperlink. While I'd not yet experienced a migraine, my symptoms don't seem to align with the health conditions related to symptoms they listed. I delete the words *head pain* from the search engine and enter the words *pain, intense, comes and goes quickly.* I start reading down through the results. After thirty minutes of searching, I sigh. Nothing I've searched seems to diagnose what I was feeling. I lean back in my chair and close my eyes. I think to myself, *Okay, just one more search.* I pinch the bridge of my nose. The pain returns. It is intense and all I can focus on and feel.

As I close my eyes, I wish it away and begin to pray. *Please, please, take this pain away.* I force myself to focus on my breathing. In and out. Breathe. In and out. Breathe. In and out. As I start focusing on my breathing, it helps me to focus on something besides the pain. I think to myself, *Why does my head hurt so badly? Where is this pain coming from?* As I continue to pray, I feel the pain slowly start to recede back into the dark place, and I begin to reflect back on the day. Fear. That was the emotion I had seen in my parents' eyes. They had both experienced loss at a young age, and now those experiences were bringing back fear of losing me. As my mind swirls with this new revelation, I can feel myself losing the battle with sleep.

The next morning, I wake up to the sun streaming through my bedroom window. As I stretch, I force my body to awaken. Rubbing sleep from my eyes, I roll out of bed and slowly put on my robe. I head down to the kitchen. The memory of the pain from the day before returns. I shudder at the thought of how intense the pain seemed to come on and how it went away so quickly.

Mom is up and moving around in the kitchen. Her eyes meet mine as I enter. She gives me a hug and then holds me back at arms' distance to look at me. She puts a hand on each side of my neck, making sure I really am okay. Her hand runs over a small bump on the side of my neck. As her hand makes contact with the bump, I exclaim, "Ow!" She pulls her hand away quickly, apologizing for causing me pain.

"When did you first notice that bump, Grace?" she asks. Puzzled, I walk to the bathroom to look at what she saw. Sure enough, there on the side of my neck just below my ear, is a small bump. I press on it again, wincing at how sore it is. A look of concern returns to my mother's face.

"I'm not sure," I respond. "I don't think it was there yesterday. If it was, it certainly wasn't painful like it is today."

My mom turns and walks out of the bathroom. Grabbing her cell phone, she calls my dad. She tells him what she is seeing, and after a short discussion, they agree that I should come to the hospital so a colleague of Dad's can take a look at my neck.

Mom is waiting for me as I come out of the bathroom. She has that worried look on her face, but despite the look of worry, she asks me about my plans for the day. The look on her face makes my stomach ache, making me unsure if my stomach hurts because I'm hungry, worried, or both. Inwardly I sigh as I think about where we are headed.

I love my dad and his coworkers. I have heard the stories my dad has shared over dinner. Dad tells stories of patients who are miraculously healed and also of those who have tragically died before their time. It is a place of such polarizing emotions. It is the mission of those who work there to help people. They give their all, day in and day out, to help those in their care.

As Mom and I walk into the hospital for my doctor's appointment, Mom's phone vibrates. It's Dad texting that he is walking to meet us. The pediatrician we are meeting with is a friend of Dad's. He has a large family, and I love to spend time with them. They are loud and fun.

We walk into his office, and I take a seat as mom chats amiably with the receptionist. She fills out the necessary paperwork, and then comes to sit down next to me. I see Dad walking into the room as Mom raises her hand to get his attention. He greets us both and then takes a seat on the other side of me. The waiting room is quiet as most of the children are absorbed in watching the animated movie playing on the television, their parents taking the opportunity to catch up on correspondence on their phones.

My parents make small talk as we wait. I don't have much to add to their conversation, so I sit quietly between them, waiting for the nurse to tell me it's my turn. Finally, the nurse emerges. She has rosy cheeks and a smile that curves wide, broadening her mouth as she smiles. She comes out with a tablet in hand, looks down, and calls my name. My parents rise, and I follow behind them. The nurse takes my weight, height, and vitals, and then she leads us to a small patient room.

While we wait for Mr. Tony, I grab one of the magazines off the wall and pretend to be busily reading. I feel comfortable with Mr. Tony. He has one of those loud, happy voices that make his Adam's apple bob up and down when he laughs. I can't help but look at it as it moves up and down, up and down. He loves to play with his kids. When I am at their home, he is the one who encourages us to go outside to play baseball, ride bikes, and make forts. Despite all I know about Mr. Tony, I can still feel my heartbeat racing as I look through the pages of the magazine. My unseeing eyes are unable to focus on any of the words or pictures. Turning the pages is keeping my hands busy and my mind focused on something other than waiting for Mr. Tony to walk through the door.

We hear a rustle outside the door. The door opens, and Mr. Tony fills most of the door frame. He pulls in a tablet on a rolling stand. My focus drifts from the rolling tablet to his face, and he smiles widely. He greets my parents with a hug, and then turns his attention to me. "Hi, Grace!" The tone of his voice matches the smile on his face. "So, my notes tell me you've been experiencing some head pain. Would you like to tell me about it?" I sigh and begin to tell him about my experiences. When I am done, I feel relieved having unburdened myself of diagnosing what is happening in my body. The other faces around me don't mirror my relief. The furrow in my mother's brow is back, and my dad and Mr. Tony have serious, stoic faces that are unresponsive to emotion. I think I'm going to have Dad teach me how to do that. My side conversation with myself is broken when Mr. Tony asks me to lay down on the patient table so he can examine me closer.

The paper crinkles, complains, and rips as I push my body back on the patient table. I sit at an elevated angle as Dr. Tony begins talking through the exam he is giving me. He starts with my feet. He asks me to take off my shoes and socks, then he helps me off the table. He asks me to stand on the floor and touch my toes. As I raise from touching my toes, he asks me to close my eyes. I see his arms on either side of me as I close my eyes, which is the last thing I remember, for after I close my eyes, I feel myself stagger to the left and then see only blackness.

Being in blackness is unique. It is quiet, peaceful, inviting even, until I start coming out of it. The light brings clarity and pain, so much pain. I bat my eyelids open and see three fuzzy heads surrounding me. My eyes. Something with my eyes. I close them again, attempting to bring the fuzzy shapes into focus. This time when I open my eyes, I see the furrowed brow of my mother, the very intense face of my dad, and the smiling face of Mr. Tony. I hear him saying, "Now there you are. Welcome back! Tell me what you are experiencing right now." I look around at the faces again as the arms around me help pull me back to a sitting position. As I begin to talk, it feels like my tongue is thick in my mouth, making it hard to speak.

Someone puts a glass of water up to my lips, and I take a couple of sips, which helps. I start to tell my parents and Mr. Tony what I just experienced. It seems like a dream. One minute I am standing up from touching my toes, and the next thing I know, I'm back on the patient table with their faces surrounding me. I had no pain until the light started to break through the darkness. Mr. Tony nods his head and then asks me if it is okay to finish his exam. After finishing his exam, he steps back by his tablet dictation stand and begins to give us his thoughts.

"I would like to order some blood work," he suggests. "What you are experiencing, Grace, is not normal for an otherwise healthy twelve-year-old girl. I'm unsure what the small bump on your neck is, but combined with head pain and blackouts, I am ordering an MRI of your head and neck." I can see my dad nodding, agreeing with Mr. Tony who continues, "After we get your test results, we'll meet up again to discuss them. Does that sound good to everyone?" He looks around at our faces as we are all nodding in agreement to his plan.

He starts dictating into the tablet the orders for the blood work and MRI. While he is speaking, he tells us where we can go to get both of these tests done. He briefly walks out of the room, grabs a few pieces of paper off the printer, and hands them to my dad. "You can take her wherever you'd like to. These are my recommendations."

My dad responds by saying, "Thank you, Tony. I think we will go downstairs and see what we can do about getting these done now." Mr. Tony nods his head, hugs both of my parents, and gives me a high five as he says his goodbyes to us.

"I'll call you when I have the results from your tests back." With that, he closes the door behind him.

My dad is the first to break the stillness by standing up from his chair. We follow him silently out of the exam room. As we walk, he pulls out his cell phone and starts making calls. During the five-minute walk from the pediatric floor to the imaging department, my dad secures both of the appointments that I need. I inwardly smile as I think to myself that I guess there are benefits to having a dad who works for the hospital.

We come in through the door that I was so excited to walk through just yesterday. Elizabeth is at the desk as we enter. News travels fast around the hospital, so I am not surprised that when our eyes meet, she hurries around the desk to give me a hug. With worry in her eyes, she tries to smile warmly and respond in like. "Hi, honey. How are you feeling?"

"Okay," I reply.

She nods her head in response and gives my mom a hug. She looks at my dad and asks, "Is it okay for me to fill your information into Grace's new patient chart? I will just need your signature."

My dad responds by nodding his head and saying, "Yes. Yes, of course, Elizabeth.

I've never been on this side of the counter before. Please, help us with this process. What else do you need?"

As Elizabeth and my dad talk through the paperwork needed to get me checked in for my procedures, Mom and I head toward a section of chairs. She steers me over near the windows that look out onto the parking lot and sits close to me. She takes my hand in her lap, and I let her. At age twelve, I'm almost too old to allow my mom to hold my hand in public, but that is not the case today. Her hand and nearness is reassuring and comforting. I lean over, resting my head on her shoulder. I am all of a sudden tired of this day.

What seems like an eternity later, my name is called. My dad greets the nurse who had called my name. Her name tag reads Brianne. She holds the door open for us as we pass by her. As the door shuts, my dad turns to us and makes the introductions.

Brianne and my dad make small talk as she leads me to a room to take my blood. She has a soft touch and before I know it, the vials of the blood needing to be drawn are full. She leaves me with a stiff piece of tape that makes it hard to bend my arm and tells me to keep pressure on it until the bleeding stops. I put my fingers over the cotton ball and tape. We say our goodbyes, heading out the door and to the right down a hallway with a shiny floor.

My dad is in the lead. He makes a few twists and turns, and we arrive outside of two double doors that say "Radiology" on them. My dad uses his hospital badge to open the doors. The people we pass by nod their hellos to Dad, their glances questioning. We pass through a door at the other end of the hallway into another waiting room. As we approach the desk, the receptionist smiles at us. She checks us in and directs us to the waiting room chairs where we can sit until my name is called for my MRI scan.

We don't sit long before I am called back. The technician performing my procedure talks me through what to expect for my MRI. While we were in the waiting room, my dad had already explained about the tube I was going to have my scan in, the knocking noise that would follow, and the cage that would be put around my head that helps the MRI machine to focus the magnet energy on my head and neck. He told me he would be in the room with me. I had nothing to fear. It won't hurt. All I have to do is hold still.

The MRI technician leads me to a small changing room and directs me to put on the top and bottom that was placed on the corner cushion of the small, curtained room. It doesn't take long for me to get changed. I look down at my trembling hands and do my best to fold my clothes into the place where the scrubs had been. My shaking hands are not working properly. I clasp my hands together and take a deep breath. Closing my eyes, I force myself to calm down. I can do this.

The MRI technician comes back to let me know he is ready. He asks me to lay down on the table. My dad moves in close to hold my hand as the technician leaves the room. I hear his voice over a speaker telling me the table will move as the scan starts. He asks me to hold still the best I can. I take a deep breath and close my eyes as the test begins.

# DIAGNOSIS
## Chapter Six

A few days after my tests are completed, Dr. Tony calls Mom and asks if it is okay for him to stop by the house later that evening. The furrow in her brow deepens, and I feel her gaze in my direction. Our eyes meet as she looks at me. She starts nodding her head first before her mouth begins to respond, "Yes, yes, of course. We will see you then." She then texts my dad to let him know Dr. Tony is planning to come by the house and to make sure to be home.

She turns to me when she gets off the phone. Her voice wavers as she begins telling me about her conversation with Dr. Tony. "Grace, Dr. Tony plans to stop by the house when he gets off work tonight. He'd like you to join us when he comes over."

I nod my head yes and reply, "Do you think he wants to give us my test results?"

"Yes," she responds, nodding her head. "Yes, I believe he does." She comes over and gives me a hug. "It's going to be fine, Grace. Whatever it is, we are in this together." As her arms come around my back, I feel my body relax against hers. I will my mind to believe what she is saying.

The day seems to drag by after the call. I finally decide to go outside and see what is happening in the neighborhood. I find my bike in the garage, wave goodbye to my mom, and am on my way. To where, I don't know, but the freedom of being away from the house and my thoughts of what is wrong with my body releases in me a new energy. A sense of freedom and invincibility starts surging through my veins.

I ride through the neighborhood as fast as I can with the wind hitting my face and whipping its fingers through my hair. The faster my legs pump the pedals around on my bike, the better I feel. As adrenaline releases into my body, I feel exhilarated. I ride as far and as fast as I can, willing my mind not to think until I start recognizing the path my body is taking me. I arrive at a trail that leads down to the lake that my parents and I fish on every summer. I throw my bike down and start running as fast as I can. My steps slow as I reach the beach. As the adrenaline begins to recede from the muscles in my body, my breathing starts to slow. I plop down on the sand and allow the sound of the lake lapping against the shore to take over my thoughts.

I sit on the beach for what seems like a long time, trying to keep away the negative thoughts. I lay back in the sand and watch the clouds float by me. Slowly the thoughts and emotions of the day start to make their way into my mind. So many thoughts. I'm unsure of what or how to feel. Fear of the unknown starts creeping to the surface again. If the tests had come back normal, Mr. Tony would've said so over the phone. Anxiety. Don't I know already that something isn't right with my body? Isn't it the fear of the diagnosis that kept me from announcing my pain for so long?

All this keeps running through my mind, like a merry-go-round that I can't stop. The pain starts creeping in from the edges of my eyes until I succumb. I grow still as I close my eyes.

I wake with a start, unsure of how long I had been laying in the sand. I look around me. A woman nearby gives me curious glances as I quickly stand up and brush the sand from my pants. I smile and nod to her and then make my way toward the trail to where my bike is waiting. My watch said I had been there for over three hours. Yikes! My mother will be worried.

The pain in my head is gone again for now, but the adrenaline I had felt earlier that day makes me feel tired and sluggish. I ride home more slowly than the speed I had when riding there. I ride past the familiar and comforting sights. Making my way past my best friend Betsy's house, I see her outside helping her mom wash their car. I stop, and Betsy makes her way over to the fence that divides the grass from the sidewalk.

"Hey, Grace!" Betsy exclaims.

"Hi, Betsy! What are you doing?" I ask.

"Helping my mom with some chores around the house," she replies.

"Do you want to come over later?" Betsy asks.

"I can't. Dr. Tony is coming over to give me my test results. Maybe tomorrow," I shrug.

"Okay!" Betsy agrees, waving as she turns and walks back to the car her mom is now wiping dry.

I ride the short distance to my house, and Mom meets me at the door. She looks at me quizzically, asking, "Where have you been, Grace?" I tell her. I tell her of all the emotions I feel, how anxious and fearful I am about something really bad being wrong with me, and how I don't want to hear what Dr. Tony has to say tonight.

She walks down the steps into the garage and wraps her arms around me. "I know. I'm scared too." She takes my hand, and we walk inside the house.

Dad arrives home early tonight, a miracle in itself. It is hard for him to get out of the emergency room. There's always one more emergency patient to attend to, but tonight the emergency patient who needs him is at home. As my dad steps into the kitchen, my mom walks to him and allows herself to be folded in against his chest. For the first time, I see the strength there--in that place of being held against his chest. I watch them for a moment before walking over to them. My dad holds out an arm and I, too, fold myself against his chest. I can hear his heartbeat steady and strong. I know in that moment that whatever is happening in my body, I will be okay because we will walk through it together.

I have never felt so bonded with and loved by my parents as I do right now. It is as if we are stronger and better together as one. The moment should've lasted longer, but the knock at the door brings us out of our embrace. Our eyes meet as Dad walks to answer the door. Mom leads me by the hand into the living room.

I sit on the chair opposite the couch where my mom sits. Dad ushers Dr. Tony to a seat on her left. Before he sits, Mom greets Dr. Tony with a hug. Dr. Tony looks at me, but my body won't allow me to move towards him, so he greets me with the nod of his head. Everything in my body is screaming to run away, but I will myself to stay and smile at him as he acknowledges me.

My parents and Dr. Tony make small talk for a few moments before Dr. Tony pulls out his tablet. He punches a few keys before getting to the screen he needs. He clears his throat and looks at my dad as he begins to talk through my test results. Some of the words he uses I have heard before, like elevated white blood cell count . . . biopsy . . . and then there was that word CANCER. I blink a few times in disbelief. I am twelve years old! How can I have cancer?

We all sit stunned to silence as Dr. Tony stands and comes over to me. He continues animatedly. It is like a horror movie. We all knew the climax was coming, but we are unable to move or speak as he continues with excitement as if he has some great secret to share. I can't help but think that he is excited that he figured out what is happening inside me. Weird.

He points to my head and references my neck, remarking, "I think the headaches you have been experiencing, Grace, were being caused by your musculoskeletal system being stressed. When you lose consciousness, it is because there is a lack of blood flow from your heart to your brain. You have enlarged lymph nodes that are pushing the muscles in your neck against your femoral artery, and I believe the reaction is resulting in the side effects you have been experiencing." He exhales and looks around at each one of our faces.

I'm not sure what he is expecting. He has just dropped a major bomb in the middle of our living room. My dad is the first to break the silence as Mom and I are still trying to find words to say. "Okay," is all that he says. He pauses to find the next words. "What's next?" he asks.

"In my opinion, our next step is get you in to see an oncologist," Dr. Tony looks at me. "An oncologist is a doctor who specializes in people who have cancer. He will help diagnose what type of cancer you have and then create a plan to help your body make the cancer go away."

All I can do is nod while tears I cannot control slip out of my eyes. My mom moves over to my chair and wraps me into her chest. She is saying comforting words to me, but all I can hear is the sound of the word cancer.

# A PLAN
## Chapter Seven

I have a biopsy at the hospital the next morning. We are all still in a state of shock about what is next and what we are to do. The biopsy is going to take a few days to come back from the lab, so Dad suggests we take the next couple of days to get out of town. I am so relieved to have something else to focus on other than my health.

Camping is one of the activities each summer I really look forward to doing with my parents. There is nothing like getting away from the city lights so I can see the much brighter lights that dazzle in the night sky. My mind goes wild imagining the shapes and designs I see in the middle of the night sky.

As we prepare our small camper with the provisions for the next few days we'll be camping, I find my joy returning at the fun I know we will have. For a moment, I almost feel normal again for the first time since the day my mom scheduled the appointment to see Dr. Tony. The smile stays on my face as I walk back and forth from the house, bringing supplies my mom wants to take with us and handing them to my dad to pack in the trailer. Dad has an incredible way of always being able to fit everything Mom wants to bring in the trailer.

As I come closer to the trailer, my dad looks up from putting the last of the dry food into one of the lower outside compartments. He smiles at me and notices, "I think that is the first smile I have seen on your face in awhile. I hope it will decide to stay for the next couple of days." My face blushes at his comment, and right then I decide that I will do my best to smile no matter how I am feeling.

Mom comes out a few moments later with the last of the items we will need for our camping adventure. My dad takes the plastic bin from her arms and loads it into the back of the truck. "That smile does look good on your face," she notices and gives me a quick side hug.

A few minutes later, we are on the road driving toward our new family adventure. Some of my first memories are of camping with my parents. It is something they've always enjoyed doing together.

When they were young, they used to camp in a tent. They tell stories of hiking down new trails together. They find great joy in discovering the new and unknown with one another. When I came into the family, they decided to purchase a small trailer, which made it easier for them to keep me safe. As I got older, my parents realized they had become accustomed to the comforts of a small trailer. They agreed they couldn't imagine going back to sleeping on the ground, or so they said.

I don't know any different and love every part of the camping trailer experience. We drive three hours northwest of our small town in northern Idaho to our favorite spot near Kettle Falls in Washington. We roll down the windows as we pull off the highway and come to a stop at the booth at the entrance of the campground. The air wafting into the car smells fresh and free.

We pay for our spot and make our way through the campground. My dad expertly backs the trailer into the space and turns off the truck. Mom and I get out and start unloading the items to make camp.

This spot is one we have been in before. The fire pit is just outside the door of the camper. It has a picnic table to the left where we eat our meals. Just beyond the end of the trailer is a small creek that leads the way to the path down to the beach at the lake.

I feel the excitement return again as we pull out each item to set up the camp for us to use for the next couple of days. It is summer, so the campground is buzzing with activity, even mid-week. We are lucky that the camp still has this space available.

After everything is unpacked and put in its new home for the next couple of days, we change into our swimsuits and head down to the beach.

The beach is a short walk down past a few other campsites, a community bathroom, and the shower areas. We follow the signs to a narrow trail that leads through the trees to the beach.

The sun glistens off the lake. I exhale as I feel the stresses of the past week melt away. Here I can just be me. Here I can soak in the sun and play until exhaustion or hunger wins.

Mom and I stake our spot on the beach while Dad walks over to a small rental shack to pay for the paddle boards we will be using that afternoon. He comes back to Mom and me and hands us each a life jacket. We walk down to the beach together, talking excitedly about the route we will take around the lake's edge. We pull our boards out into the water and start paddling around the west side of the lake. The homes on the lake are all different sizes and shapes, each one unique. As we paddle by them, we talk about what we like and don't like in each one. The conversation helps to distract my mind from my shoulder muscles that are complaining from paddling.

We reach about the halfway point around the lake and sit down on our boards to take a break. We let our legs dangle over the sides into the water. The water feels cool against my sun-warmed skin.

As I look around, I see that just a few boats are on the lake right now. My eyes wander back and forth over the shore as my parents' conversation is drowned out by the gentle lapping of the water on the shore nearby.

Something catches my attention. Someone is bending over on the beach. His back is to me, but I can tell it is a boy. From this distance it is hard to tell what he is doing. Curiosity causes me to lean forward, wondering what has caught his attention in that spot. Is he doing yard work? Maybe he is giving attention to a small animal just out of my line of sight. Or maybe he is burying something that he doesn't want anyone else to discover. My imagination starts to run wild with all sorts of different scenarios and possibilities.

All of a sudden, almost as if he senses the eyes that now bore into his back, he turns his head, and his gaze meets mine. I briskly look away. The quick movement of my head and body causes the paddleboard to tip to one side. Before I am able to counterbalance the board, my arms go above my head, and I find myself splashing into the water. As I surface, I feel my dad's arms reaching down to pull me up to my board.

"Are you okay?" Dad asks. "What happened?"

"I lost my balance and accidentally fell in. I'm okay. Really," I smile, looking both of my parents in the eye.

I sheepishly look back toward the boy on the beach. His full attention is on what had just happened in the water. He smiles and waves at us. We wave back. I can't believe I was caught! I can feel my face flush red. The color extends down my neck to my chest. My parents have no idea. I am just responding to a friendly wave from a passerby, but the boy and I share a knowing glance as I quickly avert my eyes from his.

I want to just paddle away and never see this boy again. Thankfully, my parents are ready to move on from this spot, so I eagerly lead the way.

That night after dinner, my parents and I walk over to the center of the campground, which is a community space for people at the campground to gather. It has a small playground, a general store for items that may have been forgotten by campers, and the main office.

My favorite place is the general store. It has a small corner with three bar stools at the counter. Behind the counter glass is ice cream. My parents and I wait in line for our turn to order. As we get up to the counter, the person scooping the ice cream turns around from washing his hands to take our order. As he turns, I recognize the boy from the beach. I inwardly groan, but with nowhere to go, I stand in place as my parents order their ice cream and make small talk with the boy from the beach.

His name tag says Pete. He smiles at me as I give him my order. Pete continues talking with my dad as he pays for the ice cream and leaves him a generous tip. My eyes make contact with his once more as we thank him and head out of the store into the warm night air to find a space to sit and eat our ice cream.

We find an old log and sit down knee to knee. As we sit, we talk about the fun of the day. We laugh and talk in ways that the last few weeks had stolen from us. Joy had been sucked out of our home, with anxiety and fear taking its place. In this moment, it feels like the fear of the unknown cancer in my body is a distant memory.

We finish our ice cream, and I offer to take my parents' trash to the garbage. As I head back from the trash can, Pete steps out of the store. Our eyes meet once again, and he calls out, "Hey! I've seen you around. My name is Pete." He looks like he wants to reach out his hand for me to shake, but instead he shoves his hands into his shorts pockets.

"Nice to meet you, Pete. My name is Grace," I reply.

My parents make their way over to us, and I introduce them to Pete. My dad mentions, "We are going to head back over to the trailer, Pete, would you like to join us?"

"Sure!" he responds. "I just got off for the night! I'd love to join you."

Over the next couple of hours, my parents and I get to know Pete. He is thirteen years old. His parents are teachers in a nearby city, and they manage the campground for the forestry service during their summer break. The house we saw him in front of is the home owned by the forestry department. They give his family use of it and a boat every summer. He has never known a summer that he doesn't remember coming up to the lake.

We roast marshmallows and make s'mores. As the flames from the fire dance and make shadows on our faces, we talk about memories of the past and plans for the future. There isn't one mention of me or my cancer. Laughter bubbles over as Pete tells a story about a hike with his parents. It was full of adventure and mishaps.

In my opinion, the night ends too soon when Pete stands and says, "Well, I had better be getting home. Thank you for the s'mores and the laughter. Good night!" With that, he heads down the road. My eyes follow the frame of his body until the darkness swallows him whole, and I can no longer see him.

Pete and I become quick friends, making the next two days go by much too fast. When he isn't helping his parents or working at the general store scooping ice cream, he shows me around the campground--new hiking places, secret caves, and swimming holes. Pete and I have fun together.

Pete stops by our campground after work one afternoon to tell my parents and me about a waterfall within hiking distance. He pulls out a map of the campground and shows my mom and dad where it is. My parents decide not to go but encourage us to hike the waterfall together. So, we head toward the trail.

This is the last afternoon of camping, and thoughts of what I am heading home to begin to creep back into the edges of my thoughts. Pete is walking ahead of me on the hike out to the waterfall, explaining to me about what we see along the way. He finally stops mid-sentence and looks back at me.

"Where are you today?" he asks. "You are here," he points to me, "but I can tell your mind is somewhere else. What's going on?"

So, I begin to tell him about my diagnosis. After I am done telling him all of it, I exhale. I can't look him in the eyes. I don't know what I'll find. So many thoughts come rushing through my mind. Will he still want to be friends? Will he be afraid of me?

This is the first time I have told someone all of it. My thoughts. My emotions. My fears. The story of these last few weeks from the beginning to the end. I feel turned inside out. Raw. All of my fears about dying are laid out between us. So many emotions I hadn't allowed myself to think of are finally exposed in that one moment.

After it is all spoken, I feel peace. I have no more feelings of being overwhelmed or having to keep it all inside. Softly, the tears begin to fall to the ground as we stand facing one another on the trail to the waterfall. I didn't realize how much emotion I had been holding inside of me.

"I'm sorry, Grace," Pete speaks softly. I wipe my eyes and look up for the first time. His kind brown eyes meet mine. Then he does the only thing that can comfort me at this moment. He takes my hand and begins to pray.

In the days following our return from the camping trip, Dad and Dr. Tony work tirelessly calling in every favor they have. They reach out to every person they know to make sure I am going to be seen and treated by the best doctors in the area. Because we live in a smaller city, that means referrals to friends of friends.

Dad comes home one night excited. His eyes are bright, and his face is flushed. I hear him come into the kitchen and enthusiastically talk to my mom about something. They both come out of the office with big smiles on their faces. My questioning eyes meet theirs.

"What is going on?" I ask them.

"We got you in to see her," my dad replies. "Got me in to see who?" I ask.

"The best pediatric oncologist in the United States, Dr. Kristina Nelles."

Mom and Dad give me the details of who she is and talk about the strategy for my care plan. We will leave in two days for Seattle, and the drive will take us six hours. My dad has arranged housing in a place that is close to the hospital in which I will be receiving treatment.

As they are talking excitedly about plans of what to pack, appointments to cancel, and people to call, Mom's eyes finally drift back to me. She comes over and puts her arm around my shoulder, reassuring me. I lean my head into her shoulder, and as I exhale, I think to myself that now the tough part begins.

# COMING HOME
## Chapter Eight

The next few days go by quickly as we say goodbye to friends and get ready for the time we will be gone. We know the treatment can take up to six weeks, so that is the amount of time we plan to be gone. By the time Saturday morning comes, we are ready to go. Dad packed the car the night before, so after breakfast, we all jump in the car and head west toward Seattle.

I sense joy, nervousness, and excitement. This mixture of emotions feels like a really good sugar high. It is exciting to be starting something new. We finally have our mission.

As we drive toward Seattle, Dad starts preparing me for what I am going to be experiencing during my treatment.

"Dad, what is it going to be like to have chemotherapy?" I ask. "I'm afraid it is going to hurt."

The only people I knew of that had cancer and were treated for it were older than I am. I saw what happened to their bodies from the outside, and it looked awful and painful. I wondered if that was what would happen to me. Would I lose my hair? Would I lose weight? Would I get sick?

Dad turns his head back to look at me and answers, "I don't know, Grace. Every person experiences different side effects. You could lose the hair on your head, your eyelashes, and eyebrows. Chemotherapy kills all of the good cells and bad cancer cells inside of you. It is not a therapy that is discriminating. But after speaking with Dr. Nelles about you, and the type of cancer that you have, this chemo and drug therapy that Dr. Nelles is trialing is what, in my medical opinion, I consider, the best chance we have to kill the cancer inside of you. I desire nothing more than to see you completely cured of this cancer."

I nod my head in agreement. This is my hope and desire as well. It is the fear of the unknown, though.

"What can you tell me about the drug therapy that Dr. Nelles is trialing?" I ask.

"Well," he says, "as I was doing my research about your cancer, Dr. Nelles' name and the innovative research she is doing kept coming up. I wanted to find the best option for you, so I called her. After we spoke, I was confident this was the right avenue of treatment for you."

His eyes meet mine in the rearview mirror before he continues. "What she does is she will remove stem cells from your body. She will then take them back to her lab where they use your stem cells to create a special injection that is unique to you and your specific kind of cancer. She takes these special injections, and after you have had a chemotherapy treatment and it has done its job in killing the good and bad cells, she will inject your stem cells directly into your bloodstream. The science and research shows the stem cells help to boost your immune system and increase your body's ability to heal itself faster. Her theory is that by repeating this process over and over again, your body will fight off the cancer more quickly. You are young and otherwise healthy, Grace. We both," my dad grabs my mom's hand, "have high hopes that this will give your body the best opportunity to fight off the cancer."

"Wow, Dad!" I say. "I had no idea. "Thank you for the time, energy, and research you've done to find the best treatment for me." I softly exhale.

Even after Dad's detailed explanation of the process it still feels like it is not really happening. I don't feel sick. I don't look sick. I don't understand so many things about this. Why me? Why now? I continue to ask myself questions--questions without answers, questions that keep me up most nights.

If there really is a God, why would he give me, a twelve-year-old girl, cancer? I'd never really done anything super terrible. Sure, I'd told an occasional lie and had been unkind to a few people, but why me? Questions lead to more questions. Questions I will never know the answers to, I suppose. Was God punishing me for things I have yet to do? It sure seemed like it.

My family isn't overtly religious. We do go to church a few times a year, usually for the holidays like Christmas, Easter, and maybe a few others. My dad usually works on the weekends, and Mom doesn't like going to church without him. I could take or leave church. Some of my friends go to the church we attend. I usually sit with them in the main service, and I often find myself doing the best I can not to fidget and try to find ways to entertain myself during the time the pastor is preaching.

As we continue west, I find my eyes becoming heavy as the miles continue to roll past. The sound of the car finally lulls me to sleep. Sleep is the only place these days I find peace. It seems the places I go in Beyond, people know my story and they look at me with those "poor you" eyes. I much prefer spending time with those who treat me normally.

Why is it that when people feel sorry for someone, the way that they compensate for it is sometimes so awkward that it leaves the sick person having to comfort the person who is saying the awkward remarks? Everywhere I went in Beyond, I was on edge. I found very few places in our town to be safe places. I was looking forward to going to a new place where no one knows my name, my story, or about my cancer. I imagine that in that place, everyone will treat me normally again.

I awake from my nap. Disorientated, I realize as I sit up that we are pulling into the driveway of the home that my parents had rented a house for us to stay in for my treatment time.

The house is white and set close to the street. Its doors and shutters are blue like the sky. The small front yard is full of lush, green grass that looks freshly mowed. It is a cute, friendly looking house within walking distance of the hospital where my treatments are to take place.

We climb out of the car. My dad opens the front door as my mom and I start grabbing our belongings out of the trunk to carry them in the house.

As I walk inside, I first notice the living room. It feels warm. The shabby furniture looks well loved, yet comfortable. As I walk down the hallway, I peek in and see the kitchen with its white subway tiles, farmhouse sink, and modern appliances. It is inviting, matching the feel of the living room.

I leave the kitchen after putting the items from my arms into the refrigerator. I head back out to the car and go back and forth until everything we had brought for our stay is safely tucked into place.

We decide to have some fun for the rest of the day. As I close my eyes that evening, I feel the day wash over me, lulling me into a dreamless night's sleep. The next day is Monday and my first day of treatment.

The next morning, Mom and Dad are already awake as I make my way downstairs. I follow my nose to find them. The scent of coffee and bacon fill the air. We have to be at the hospital by 9 a.m., and my parents want to arrive early to make sure everything is in place for me. They have me sit, eat, and then shoo me upstairs to shower and dress.

Arriving at the hospital in plenty of time before my appointment, we head toward reception, my dad taking the lead. He starts talking with the receptionist whose name tag read Cathy. "Good morning, Cathy," he greets. "We are here to see Dr. Nelles. This is my daughter Grace. We are going to be seeing you often over these upcoming weeks." He smiles at Cathy. Building rapport is something my dad does well. He is well received by his co-workers because he takes the time to get to know them, their families, and their hobbies.

"How long have you worked here at Waverly Hospital?" Dad asks Cathy.

"I've worked here for over ten years," she replies. The conversation between my dad and Cathy continues for a few minutes more, during which time we find out that Cathy is in her forties, or at least that's what I calculate. She has olive skin and straight black hair that hangs down to her shoulders. When she smiles, her brown eyes fold under her black lashes and create a crescent shape that makes me smile. She has two teenage children that she is obviously very proud of, by the way she speaks of them. Her husband works for Waverly Hospital, as well, in the IT department.

Cathy gives us directions to Dr. Nelles' office, and we wave our goodbyes to her as we head in the direction she has pointed us. Mom joins hands with Dad as we head to the elevator. I sense that as we are nearing the place we are going to be spending most of our time over these next weeks, Mom needs the weight of support that my dad's hand provides. I stand in the elevator, wishing for the first time I had a friend with me--someone who can distract me. I think back on our camping trip and of Pete, when the ding of the elevator sounds the arrival to our destination and brings my thoughts back to the present.

As we make our way off the elevator, my eyes are met with bright colors and smiling faces. The white walls of the hospital have been transformed into a jungle from the walls to the ceiling. Everywhere I look are murals of lush trees and smiling animals. As I stand and wait for my parents to check me in, I allow my eyes to slowly cover every square inch of the area.

It is not what I expected, but I suppose I am not quite sure of what I did expect. Treatment is a word that sounds scary to me. I am not sure what the rest of the hospital looks like, but this floor is not scary. It is filled with joy. Interesting. Interesting, indeed.

A nurse walks down the hallway. Smiling, she asks us to follow her. She leads us down a colorful hallway. I look back and forth at the different murals on the walls around me. The nurse steps back from a door that is surrounded by tall trees with hanging vines. Happy-looking monkeys are hanging on the vines that usher us into a small exam room.

The nurse asks me to sit. She takes my temperature and vitals and says that Dr. Nelles will be in shortly to see me. I respond by saying, "Thank you." She smiles and leaves.

A few minutes later, Dr. Nelles enters. My dad stands and greets her with a hearty, friendly, colleaguely-type hand shake. My eyes run over her face. Her eyes catch my attention. She has kind eyes that meet mine before her attention moves from my dad to me. She reaches out her hand and greets me. "Hi, Grace, my name is Dr. Nelles. You and I are going to be working together to help your body fight the cancer."

# THE TREATMENT
## Chapter Nine

The treatment will begin the next day. Dr. Nelles suggests we go and get a good lunch and do something fun together for the remainder of the day, for none of us knows what the days ahead will hold.

My parents take me to my favorite restaurant--a fun place full of life and fried food. They tell me to order whatever I want off the menu, so I do. I am only able to eat half of what I ordered, and my parents and I laugh and tell stories we recall from the past when my stomach had also encouraged me to order more food than what I was able to eat.

My heart and belly are full as we leave the restaurant and get back in the car. My parents then surprise me by taking in the summer's blockbuster movie. It is truly a perfect day.

The next morning begins early. We wave hello to Cathy as we walk past the reception area in the lobby of the hospital. We walk quickly to the bank of elevators. All three of us are nervous about what is to come today.

As we exit the elevator, a nurse meets us and leads us the opposite way down the hall. She has me sit in a comfortable chair in a room that has an IV stand next to its arm. My parents sit close to me on a couch to my left. As the nurse prepares my arm to receive the first treatment, she talks me through each step.

My first chemotherapy treatment is not as I thought. It is easy to sit in a chair, watch tv, and play games on my device. The hardest part of the treatment is the length of time that it takes. The thought of doing this three times a week for the next couple of weeks bores me to no end.

I feel fine after the first day and the night. The chemotherapy drug they put in doesn't make me feel sick until the end of the week.

I awake after the third treatment, on a Saturday morning, to the sound of my body trying to throw up the previous night's dinner and dessert. I run to the bathroom connected to my room. My mom meets me there to soothe me and hold my hair. We sit on the floor until the throwing up subsides. Then she and my dad help me back to bed.

Over the second week, what I saw from others who had undergone chemotherapy came true. I have lost my appetite from nauseousness, and the hair on my head begins to fall out in clumps. I begin the trial drug, which Dr. Nelles tells me I am tolerating well.

Dr. Nelles tells my parents what to look for in my health. She gives us a list of suggestions that can help. My mom leaves before my treatment is over for the day to collect the items that Dr. Nelles says I should have on hand.

By the end of the second week, I am down three pounds. I have patches on my head where my hair is thinning. I know not what the third week will hold, but I shudder at the thought.

The beginning of the third week, Dr. Nelles starts by saying that my body is holding up well. This treatment is meant to be intense and pervasive. My dad and her both agree that aggressive is the best way to treat and kill the cancer in my head and my body.

The pain from headaches comes back in the third week. It causes concern from my dad and Dr. Nelles. They decide to order more tests, which are to be done after my treatments that day.

The tests they want to run are a PET scan and more blood work. By the end of that week, we have the test results back. The cancer in my head is not responding to the treatments. My white blood cell count is dangerously low. Instead of shrinking, the masses in my head are growing. Both my parents and Dr. Nelles are discouraged. They spend the rest of my treatment time that day coming up with another course of action for me and my cancer.

The fourth week, my treatment plan changes. The chemotherapy stops, and I will begin radiation. My dad tells me that they are surprised at how fast-growing my cancer is. Their thought now moves from healing it completely to slowing down the rate of the cancer's growth. The radiation treatment area is in a different part of the hospital. They take me by wheelchair from the jungle floor to an area that is sterile with white walls. My body begins to receive the radiation treatments.

Later that night, I awaken to something warm and sticky coming out of my nose. It takes great effort for me to push out of bed and make my way to the bathroom. I turn the light on and find to my great surprise that blood is coming out of my nose. I yell out to my parents, unsure of what to do, as fear rises up in the pit of my stomach.

My parents run in and find me hunched over the sink, blood pouring out of my nose uncontrollably. My mom tries to use toilet paper to pinch off the flow of blood. My dad gets his phone to call Dr. Nelles who recommends that they bring me right in to the hospital emergency room, and she will meet us there.

My parents rush me into the emergency room at the hospital. The emergency room staff is efficient, but the way they work with me feels different. I look at my mom's face and see the line between her eyes deepen as they struggle to get the bleeding under control.

At Dr. Nelles' direction, the emergency room staff cauterizes the bleeding in my nose. The bleeding finally stops. I close my eyes, exhaling with relief. She orders them to admit me and run more tests to find out the source of the bleeding.

A few hours later, I am back on the floor with the brightly colored jungle animals painted on the walls. My room is full of bright colors and is happy and joyful despite what is happening inside of me. As my gaze scans around the room, my eyes fall on my parents, both resting now on the makeshift beds the hospital has provided.

I smile as I think to myself how thankful I am to have them as my parents. I close my eyes and drift off into the first dreamless, painless sleep.

I awake the next morning to the sound of the door to my room opening. Keeping my eyes closed, I hear footsteps across the floor and the sound of Dr. Nelles' voice quietly talking. I hear her say, "There is not much more we can do. I'm so sorry, but the cancer has grown to the point where I don't have any more treatment options."

Mom begins to cry softly. Dad begins to argue that there must be more we can do. I hear him plead, "She is young and otherwise healthy. Is there someone else who can help?"

I open my eyes to see Dr. Nelles' face. She looks defeated and tired. It must take a toll on her when she can't heal and help the children in her care. They look over at me and realize I am awake. They walk over to the side of the bed, coming over to gently explain the conversation I had just overheard. I exhale, close my eyes, and quietly say, "I want to go home."

# FINAL DAYS
## Chapter Ten

As we drive home from Seattle to Idaho, Mom makes many phone calls to prepare the house for my return. I am not coming back the same as I had left. When I left, I was full of hope that the treatments in Seattle were going to heal my body, and I would return with a great story and with no cancer.

Unfortunately for me, that is not my story. Instead of being cured from cancer, I am coming home in need of care that I had not previously needed. The phone calls continue the entire drive as my mom has to order all the items Dr. Nelles said I needed to continue my care at home.

As I walk through the front door of our home, I stop. I see my reflection in the entryway mirror. Staring back at me is a stranger. I had an image in my mind of what I look like, and the person in the mirror is not me.

The person in the mirror has lost most of the hair on her head. While she still has her eyelashes and eyebrows, it is a strange look. The image in the mirror has my eyes and face.

I put my hand on the frame of the front door as I run my hand over the curve of my head. This is new. I had never known the shape of my head. I turn my head side to side, getting a good look at the image staring back in the mirror. My body is thin. The previous weeks' treatments have taken their toll. My clothes hang loosely over my thin body. Food has lost its taste, and the medications have stolen my appetite. Even the food I once loved doesn't sound good to me now. My parents work hard to get me to eat. They buy me all of the foods that I love in an attempt to keep up my weight. I would take a few bites to lessen the worry on their faces, but the weight loss continued.

The dark circles under my eyes stand out blue and purple against my pale skin. Another side effect of the treatments is my sensitivity to light. It hurts my eyes and my head to be outside, so I instead prefer to be inside to make the pounding in my head lessen. As I stare at the person in the mirror, I think to myself, "Who is this stranger?" I sigh and move past the mirror into the living room that has been transformed into my temporary bedroom.

I am too weak now to climb the two flights of stairs up to my bedroom, and with all the equipment needed to care for me, my parents think it best to bring my bedroom downstairs. An army of people from the community rallied to help. It looks so much like my bedroom that I feel myself immediately relax despite the new additions of medical equipment curiously hidden among what I love.

I sit down on the bed. My mom comes and sits beside me to help me take off my shoes. Even the little tasks like pulling my shoes on and off are difficult for me now.

Bending down, no matter how I try, brings the blood rushing to my head and increases the pounding inside my brain. It doesn't take me long to realize I need help, even with the simplest tasks. So, despite the desire I have to do for myself, I am resigned to need help.

I can see that my mortality is in jeopardy. I'm unsure why I thought that the treatment in Seattle was going to be a quick fix. It may have been because of my age or underlying hope. Why did I have so much hope? I don't feel hopeful now. I feel defeated. Alone. Ugly. The treatments hadn't been kind to me. All I want to do is close my eyes, shut it all out, and make the thoughts and the pain go away. So, I do. I slip into a dreamless sleep.

The next day, I wake to the light streaming through the windows at the front of the house. It takes me a moment to acclimate myself to where I am. Home! I am at home! Being at home is wonderful! I am immediately thankful to be back in our home. I take in a deep breath. The stabbing pain in my head is still there.

My reality comes rushing back with the last words from Dr. Nelles. "Terminal.

Inoperable. There is nothing else we can do. Keep her comfortable and enjoy the time you have left with her is what I suggest for you to do. She could have two weeks, or she could have two months. It is hard to exactly tell. This cancer is more aggressive than what I first thought. I'm so sorry," explained Dr. Nelles.

I hear someone making his way down the stairs. I make an attempt to sit up in bed, which is not a good idea, so I sigh and flop my head back down on the pillow. My dad, seeing the end of my attempt, rushes over, props the pillows up, and says, "I'm glad you are up! I have some things to discuss with you before your mom comes down." I sit up a little straighter.

As he starts to talk, he begins to get teary. Apologizing, he continues to talk to me about my diagnosis. He shares his thoughts and then asks me, "What do you want, Grace?"

I look at him, not sure what to say. This is the first time somebody has asked me what I want. I pause for a moment before responding, "I don't want to be in pain, and for as long as I can, I want to be around friends and family."

His mouth smiles, but his eyes are sad. I reach out my hand and softly say, "It's going to be okay, Dad." He closes his eyes and hangs his head. I feel a wave of emotion rolling over him. For the first time in my life, I feel I have a purpose. I can encourage him. From out of the brokenness of my body swells a desire to leave behind joy and hope.

What will we leave behind when we are gone from this earth? Some call it a legacy. For me, I feel like I have a new purpose. It is all so perfectly clear. I will leave those around me better for knowing me.

No longer will I let the pain define me. I choose to live each day in the best way I can.

In much pain, I sit up, swinging my legs over the side of the bed to place my feet on the ground. I lean over and give my dad a hug. He wraps his arms around me and begins, "I'm so sorry I couldn't help you, Grace. I'm so sorry. I'm so sorry. I'm so sorry!"

Pain. I am in physical pain, but my dad is in emotional pain. He is feeling defeated. It's something I'm unsure he had ever faced. Although my body is being defeated from cancer, and I sit here in pain, broken from the inside out, I have something to give--hope.

"Dad, it is going to be okay. I'm going to be okay," I comfort him. "There is nothing that can keep me from where I am going. My life has been bought with the blood of Jesus. When it is my time to go from my pain, I am going to a place where I will live again with Jesus. You will see me again."

His breathing slows, as does his crying. He looks up at me and breathes, "Thank you, Grace."

Wow! Where did that come from? Something I had heard years ago resounded in my ears. There is power in the name of Jesus. He is a peace that passes all understanding. My dad had come to me to bring me comfort, but instead, something inside of me stirred with compassion, desiring to bring him peace and hope. I didn't understand it, but I was going to continue to use it and speak it.

"Dad, I want to invite people here. Anyone who wants to see me. I don't know how much time I have." My voice falters. I finally speak the words that had only been conversed in my head, and for the first time, I feel my reality, my final reality, really registering. I don't feel anxiety or fear. All I feel is peace.

# THE MIRACLE
## Chapter Eleven

Having heard what I had to say and why I was making this request, my dad helps me make a list of all the people I want to see, and then we set to work reaching out to each person. I use my phone to text those I know. Mom and Dad call those who don't receive texts or who are too far away to make a visit and need to schedule a time to talk to me by phone. By the time we are all done, we have contacted over sixty people in all.

I smile as I think about the days and weeks to come. I have something to look forward to, finally. My mom and dad tape my visitor calendar to the wall next to my bed in the living room. Since I can't go to each of the people we had called or texted, I am relieved that people are willing to come to me.

I am still unsure what I will say or how these conversations will go, but I look forward to each one, just wanting the opportunity to bring hope.

I draw a picture of the word *hope*. I make the letters of the word broad and wide using different colors to highlight the curve and shape of each letter. I accentuate the letters with flowers, hearts, dots, and sparkly stickers. When I finish with the project, I am exhausted but more than satisfied with my effort. Mom puts it up on the wall at the foot of my bed so I can stare at it.

HOPE. There is no physical hope for my body now, but I can leave those around me with the hope I feel inside of me. I silently pray that I will have the opportunity to share the hope inside me with each person who visits. I am not sure what exactly that is going to look like, but I am excited for the chance to speak to, spend time with, and bring hope to each one. I realize it is the people in our lives that are our treasures. Relationships leave a mark, and I want to leave a mark on the people I know.

## MY FIRST VISITOR

My first visitor comes early the next morning. I can hear her breathing heavily as she enters. "I'm so sorry to be late," the voice apologizes. I don't have to see her face to know it is my best friend Betsy. I smile when I hear her voice. I have missed Betsy. I close my eyes, and my mind drifts back to times of laughter, fun at school, and sleepovers.

I am smiling as she walks in the room. She has a curious look on her face, which I immediately realize is in response to seeing me lying with my eyes closed in the bed in the living room. I laugh, and Betsy laughs too. It is just what we need to break the ice. She sits next to me in a comfortable chair that my parents have arranged next to the bed. Betsy has a bag with her. As she sits, she starts pulling out some paper. She has my full attention as she places all hand-drawn, beautiful cards on the bed. There were so many!

Betsy tells me that friends from school and people who had heard my story started making cards for me, but because I hadn't been home, Betsy offered to gather and keep them until I returned. We spend the next couple of hours reading through each card.

Betsy remarks on some of them that had stories to accompany the card. As we read through them, I ask her to tape them on the wall around the hope sign I had made. When she is done, I have an amazing, colorful collage of hope and encouragement.

I smile at the wall, thanking Betsy for helping put it together. She joins me on the bed, and we both sit back and laugh as the bed groans with the weight of both of us.

She takes my hand, and looking at the word *hope* at the end of the bed says, "I'm so sorry, Grace."

"Me too," I reply. "This isn't the way I thought this would go." "Are you scared?" she asks.

"I was, but I don't feel scared anymore. I feel hope," I remark as I look at the wall.

"Hmm," is all she says as she nods her head.

I'm not sure how much Betsy really does understand, but sometimes best friends don't need to fully understand one another. I lean my head on her shoulder. "Thank you for coming today. Will you come again?"

"If it is okay with you, I would like to come every day."

I smile and nod my head. "That is what I was hoping you'd say."

Over the following weeks, Betsy keeps her word. She comes every day. If I am with someone else, she waits until we are done before coming in to spend time with me. She continues to bring cards she's collected from people in the community. She fastens each card to the wall with tape as she comes in for each visit.

## ELIZABETH

Elizabeth from the hospital is at the door, and I am excited to see her. She comes in the evening after work, still in her scrubs. As I lean over the bed, I can see her hugging both of my parents. My dad has taken time off from the hospital to tend to my care. He now is my primary doctor and caregiver, and Mom assists him.

"How is she?" Elizabeth asks.

"She has good days and not-so-good days. She is having a not-so-good day today. So, if you would keep your visit brief, she can rest. She is needing much more rest these days."

I hear the sound of defeat and sadness again in his voice. As they make their way into my room, Dad says to Elizabeth something that he and Mom together have already discussed with me. My body is beginning to slow down. It's expected, my dad had said.

"Okay," Elizabeth says. "I brought her some things that I thought we could work on together if she is up for it."

I hear the positivity in my mom's voice as she replies, "Oh, Elizabeth, these are wonderful! Thank you for thinking of her!"

Elizabeth tells my dad just how much he is missed at work. He smiles and says, "Thank you, Elizabeth. That means a lot. Please give everyone my regards, and update them on what is happening with Grace."

She finally makes her way to the side of the bed. The look on her face is a combination of worry and joy. She pauses before sitting down, and it is almost as if the emotions inside her are at war, trying to decide which one will lead. I smile, hoping my gesture gives her the freedom to leave behind her worry. She gives me a hug, pushing the hair off my forehead, still without saying a word. She opens her bag, and I lean over to see the surprise she has brought me. She pulls out a purple cloth bag with a gold drawstring. She reaches in and pulls out something beautiful. It is glass pieces all faceted precisely like I've seen in a hanging chandelier.

As she holds this up, the light begins to shine through it, casting rainbows on the wall. "You've always been so thoughtful, thinking of me when making your wonderful art pieces, that I thought I would bring you something that I've been working on. Hopefully it will bring some sparkle to your space."

She lays the beautiful, tiered glass prisms on my lap so I can touch them with my fingertips. I look up and breathe, "This is beautiful! Thank you!"

"Where would you like me to hang it?" she asks.

We spend the next few minutes trying to decide the best place for the glass prisms to hang that will catch the most light. When we find the perfect spot, Elizabeth wraps the clear line on the top of the prisms around a thumb tack and pushes it up into the drywall in the ceiling.

"Perfect!" she declares, and I have to agree. The light reflects through all the glass with a beautiful effect. She hurries back over and starts pulling more items out of her bag--sealed plastic bags full of glass prisms, pliers, fishing line, and hooks to hang and piece them together.

"Want to make another?" she asks. I can barely contain my excitement. I cannot believe she has brought all of these glass prisms for us to string together. I nod my head and smile. She sets to work showing me how to connect the prisms together. I sit criss-cross applesauce so I can lay out my design before stringing it together. Elizabeth gives me some direction, and then we set to work.

We carefully attach and pinch together silver rings into each hole in the top of the glass prisms. Then we tie a clear fishing line to each one, knotting each ring securely to the prism. My hands are unsteady as we get close to being done, so she offers to help me finish mine after she has completed hers.

We hold up our finished work. The light dances through the glass, making beautiful colors on the light-colored shirt I am wearing.

"When did you start making these, Elizabeth?" I ask.

"I found this box of glass prisms at a garage sale a few years ago. They looked like they didn't have a purpose any longer after being removed from the chandelier they once graced, but I had this thought. 'What if I could make something from them?' One person's trash is another person's treasure!" she laughs at herself.

"You know," I say, "I've seen you do that quite often. You see the potential in things and people in a way other people do not. That is a gift."

She looks at me and dabs her eyes a few times as she replies, "Thank you, Grace. I needed to hear that today." She grabs my hand and squeezes it, continuing to try and blink the tears from coming off the sides of her eyes.

Before leaving, Elizabeth hangs our new prisms up on the ceiling. My hope wall is now sparkling, thanks to the prisms from my friend Elizabeth.

Pointing to the box that she'd brought with all the supplies for the prisms she says, "I'll leave these for you until I return to visit next. I hope to see many more prisms when I return for the box," she smiles.

"Thank you!" I exclaim. Elizabeth gives me a hug and leaves the room. Her presence lingers with the reflection of the light through the glass making rainbows on the walls.

Mom comes in after Elizabeth leaves and sits with me on the bed. She sweeps the hair from my face, tucking it behind my ear. We sit in silence for a moment, admiring the wall in front of us.

"This is incredible!" Mom responds.

"I know!" I agree. "Isn't it amazing? It brings a whole different light to hope," I say smiling. I gesture to the wall covered in cards with encouraging words, my sign with the word *hope,* and now the rainbow of colors dancing across it all with the light from the prisms hanging on the ceiling.

"Hungry?" she asks.

"No," I reply. "I think I'll just sit here enjoying the beauty of the show."

"Okay," she says, kissing my forehead. She pulls me in close, and I lean my head on her chest. I feel my eyes getting heavy. She begins to run her fingers through my thinning hair. I close my eyes and rest in her arms.

There is still one person my parents and I have not seen. He is someone I am looking forward to seeing. He's a newer friend I've made ... Pete.

Neither my parents nor I are sure when he'll come. With cell service intermittent and Pete's parents' commitments to the campground, they are unsure when they will be able to come into town. So, I decide to write him a letter.

*Dear Pete,*

> *I'm so happy I met you camping this summer. I still laugh at my embarrassment when I think back to the first time that I saw you.*
> *Thank you for showing me around the campground. Next summer when I come up, you are going to have to be ready to show me some more cool places around the area.*
> *I really think you should think about being a tour guide some day. You are really good at pointing out things of interest. I'm thankful that just after meeting me you discerned enough about me to choose places you knew I would like to see.*
> *You could have your own business every summer, or something like that.*
> *I hope this letter finds you having a grand adventure. I know that is how I will remember our time at camp together.*

*Until we see each other again,*
*Grace*

It has been over a month since I have gotten home from Seattle. We have people coming and going on most days. Sunday is the only day we don't have visitors, and we spend time together as a family. The visitors begin to stay for shorter and shorter periods of time, as I am more tired these days. It is getting harder for me to focus on conversation. My dad says that is normal. He suggests that if I eat more than a few bites a day, I may feel like I have more energy to focus on my words of hope for each visitor as I had planned.

I hear what he says, but my body says otherwise. Every time I eat, my stomach gets queasy, and I feel nauseous. It's a side effect of the pain medication, my dad has told me. It keeps the pain in my head away, but it suppresses my appetite so that I don't feel hungry.

Their concern is not unfounded. I am noticeably thinner this week. Today is my weekly check in, which is something my dad started to record each week to indicate how my body is doing. The check in consists of him taking my temperature and blood pressure, listening to my lungs, and checking my weight. My mom helps by sitting in a nearby chair and recording the numbers my dad reads.

When it is time to take my weight, Dad helps me off the bed to the floor where he has brought the scale from their upstairs bathroom. Last week when I had weighed in, I weighed a little less than I had been the week before, but that was to be expected with my erratic ability to eat. At this check in, I weigh ten pounds less than I had last week!

My dad can't believe his eyes. He asks me to step off the scale and then back on three separate times to confirm the weight that registers on the scale. He looks up at me as he crouches next to the scale and pleads, "Please, Grace, your body can't continue to sustain this type of weight loss. Your body will get too weak and . . ." his voice falters "and you will die." He can't even look at me when he says it, but it hits me hard. As he helps me back into bed, he kisses my cheek and leaves the room. The impact of his words makes the pounding in my head return with a new fervor.

"Mom," I say with my eyes closed.

"Yes, Dear," she replies.

"Can I have something for the pain?" I ask.

"It's not quite time, but I suppose. Let me go and get your dad so he can give it to you," she responds.

She leaves the room to get my dad to administer the pain medication. I lean down to grab my water glass, and as I reach, the momentum of my body propels me to my side, causing me to roll out of bed and hit the floor with a thud. As my body takes the impact of my fall, I feel something inside of my head burst! I feel pain. I see light and then blackness.

I hear my parents' shouts, then the sounds of sirens. I sense I am no longer at home but instead in a new place. I must be dreaming. My dreams never make sense, but this one has a quality of reality that instead of waking to it, draws me into experiencing it more.

This new place I am in is so bright. I sense an urgency around me, but all I feel is peace. I look up and within the light is an outstretched hand. I place my hand into the one offered to me and see a face. It is a kind face. His eyes are tender. The curve of his lips is inviting. I can see his lips moving, but the words don't have sound. I lean in, straining to hear him. "I'm sorry," I hear myself say, "I cannot hear what you are saying."

"It's not time for you yet. Go back and tell them all the things you have seen. Build and share the hope you have found. Look for me. I want to be found."

As soon as the last word is spoken, the light subsides into blackness again.

# LIFE AFTER
## Chapter Twelve

Beep. Beep. Beep. The steady beeping noise continues. I wonder why no one is turning off the sound. I try to look around to find where the noise is coming from and find it difficult to move. I must be dreaming, I rationalize. Why else can I not see anything but the darkness around me?

For the first time in many months, I realize my head doesn't hurt. I try to move my hand to feel my head, but I cannot move my hand. I wonder if it is that I don't move my hand or if I cannot move my hand. I am not sure. I can't see my hand through the darkness to confirm.

I hear a faint, familiar voice coming from somewhere in the darkness calling my name. "Grace! Grace! Can you hear me? It's Mom. Please, try and come back to me."

Weird. Why is Mom asking me to come back to her? I can't see her, but the sound of her voice is getting closer and closer. Light. I can see more light now. It is faint at first but seems to be getting brighter.

Curious. This blackness I am in is so comforting and peaceful--a place I am rather enjoying. The light is persistent and grows brighter and brighter and brighter until I have to close my eyes because it is so intense.

"She blinked!" I hear my dad say. Of course I blinked. An incredibly bright light is shining in my eyes. "Grace, if you can hear me, open your eyes." I do.

I have to blink more than a few more times to help my eyes focus on what is around me. The first item I see is my hope sign with all of the cards surrounding it, but that is all that is familiar. This room is small. The walls are white, and I can now see the machine causing the steady beeping sound I'd heard. The finger of my left hand has a clip on it that allows the machine next to my bed to keep track of my heart rate.

My hands. I can see them now that the darkness is gone. I look up and see my dad standing behind Mom's chair. They are both smiling at me. My mom grabs my right hand and cries, "I knew you'd come back to us!"

Come back to them? Where did I go? When did we get separated? Where am I? I can feel the crease in my brow furrow, like my mother's does when she is concerned. I begin to think of all the questions I have surrounding that one statement.

My dad runs out of the room, and I hear shouts of excitement. Still unsure of what is going on, I look at my mom. She smiles, "You've been asleep for awhile. Dad went to alert the staff. We want to make sure you are okay now that you are awake. This is so exciting!" she exclaims, kissing me on the hand.

Dad comes back into the room, pulling a machine. A line of people follow him. He comes over to the opposite side of the bed to Mom. He reaches out and hugs me. "I'm so thankful you are awake!" He looks at my mom and asks, "Has she said anything yet?" Still smiling, my mom shakes her head no.

I haven't had the opportunity to talk. Since the brightness of the light forced me to open my eyes, there had been so much to take in around me that I haven't thought to speak aloud the questions I am conversing in my head.

My dad begins talking to the people who had followed him into my room. "Grace, meet my interns here at the hospital. They are here to learn how to connect this machine to your brain and help monitor its activity. I'm going to ask you some questions, and I want you to tell me the answers. Okay?" I nod my head.

"Good!" he replies. "Okay, let's start with some easy ones. What is your name?"

I can hear myself answer his question with the correct answer, "Grace," but no movement or sound comes from my mouth in response. The machine Dad had connected to my head makes a spike as I continue to say my name over and over again in my head without being able to verbalize the word.

I begin to panic, looking back and forth between my parents. I don't understand what is happening to me. I've never not been able to speak. What happened to me when I was in the darkness?

My parents look at each other, and I know something is wrong. I begin to cry. My dad breaks the silence, "Everyone out, please." The line of interns quickly exit at his request. "Let's give Grace some space. I think we need to tell her what has happened over the past six months."

"You're right," Mom agrees. Turning to me, she asks, "What do you last remember, Grace?"

My voice is just a whisper, but I am able to answer. "I remember being at home in bed. My head was hurting," my voice falters. "Something happened. I felt an explosion in my head. There was so much pain. I remember hearing voices I recognized. I heard shouts. The sound of an ambulance. More shouting. Bright lights, and then there was this peace that came to me when a man in white appeared. He spoke to me." I shake my head. That part was fuzzy as well. "Then he left. When he left, he took the light with him, and there was nothing but the darkness until now."

I look up into the faces of my parents. They are leaning into the bed, holding hands. "That's incredible, Grace!" my dad exclaims. "Our experience was quite different." He proceeds to tell me that they heard a sound after leaving me that had them hurrying back to find the cause. They found me on the floor by my bed, a small trickle of blood coming from my nose.

"We were so scared, Grace! We didn't know what had happened to you. We just saw the blood," Mom explained.

Dad continues, "The shouting you told us you heard was probably us panicking around you. Me trying to keep you stable and yelling over to Mom to tell the 911 operator what was happening." He takes a deep breath, "You had stopped breathing." He pauses, looking for the words to continue.

Mom begins to tell the story now. "Dad worked furiously, trying to get you breathing again. It seemed like an eternity before the ambulance arrived to take over. Dad went with you in the ambulance, and I followed in the car. They rushed you into the emergency room. Dad had called ahead, and his team was ready for you. You needed to be quickly intubated." She moves her hand to the scar that remains just above my collar bones.

I reach up to feel the new scar between my collar bones and smile.

"Grace, you like the thought of having a new scar," my mom notices. I smile again.

She laughs, and my dad smiles as well. I am going to have a cool story to tell.

Mom continues. "After they had stabilized your breathing, they sent you to have a Cat Scan. The CT scan showed that there was an aneurysm in your brain."

Dad interrupts, "An aneurysm is a blood vessel that bursts."

Mom continues, "They still don't understand how you are still alive." She shakes her head back and forth. "They did not give you a good prognosis but recommended they go in to stop the bleeding." My mom stops talking. She looks at my dad, and he continues on with the story.

"Like Mom said, you were not expected to make it, but we wanted to give you every opportunity to live. So, we agreed--you would rather die fighting." My eyes meet his. He knows me so well. I smile again, trying to confirm the words he is saying.

"Thank you for confirming our decision, Grace," Dad says as he pats my hand. I try to move my fingers to touch his hand, and they won't move. "They rushed you into the operating room where they spent many hours trying to stop the bleeding in your brain.

The cancer nodules in your brain, the surgeon told me afterwards, helped absorb the blood as they worked. He said he had never seen anything like it. The masses were almost like sponges in your brain, keeping the blood from spreading beyond the areas they were working in to stop the bleeding." He shrugs and shakes his head side to side. "After they successfully stopped the bleeding, they carefully removed two of the three masses of cancer.

"Did you experience or see anything else while you were asleep, Grace? The reason I ask is that, according to the surgeon's notes, you died on the operating table. They successfully resuscitated you, but we were unsure if you would wake up after all of the trauma your brain experienced. And if you did wake up, what effect that would have on your body. You've been unconscious for over three months now."

I smile.

"It is truly a miracle, Grace! Sometimes medicine cannot explain the miracles we see. I know for sure as Mom and I sit here telling you this story, that you are a miracle. I can't explain medically how you are sitting here alive with us now," his voice falters as tears come to his eyes. "We are so thankful you are still here with us."

He looks over at the door as a woman enters. I have never seen her before, but as she comes in, she smiles at me and begins to talk. Her voice is so familiar. "Hello, Grace! It is so nice to see you awake! My name is Dr. Epstein, but you can call me Carol." I smile at her. "I'm happy to see you can hear me and respond." She looks at my parents and asks them, "Has she spoken yet?"

"Yes," my dad answers. "I'm unsure if she can move."

"Okay," Carol replies. "Grace, are you okay if I test your body's reflexes?" she asks. I smile in agreement with her question.

She walks to the door and calls a nurse to come into the room. She asks the nurse to take notes, and she begins. "Let's start with your eyes, Grace." She shines a small flashlight back and forth into each of my eyes. "Looks great! Your pupils are reacting normally." She smiles at me, and I smile back in response. She spends the next ten minutes testing the reflexes from my eyes down to my feet.

As she moves to each body part that she tests, she asks me different questions. She asks me to smile if I can feel, and I am able to smile at each part. My body's reflexes seem to be responding as they should, which Carol says is all good news.

When she is done examining me, she asks Dad and Mom if they would like to step out of my room with her for a few moments. They nod their heads. My mom pats my leg and assures me, "We will be right back, Grace." I nod in agreement.

Whatever Dr. Epstein has to say about me is not something she is ready to share with me. I roll my eyes as I wonder why adults always think they need to protect.

My parents come back to my room, and I smile. They sit back down, each putting a hand on me. Dad begins "Dr. Epstein, umm Carol, said you have a tough road of recovery ahead of you, Grace. Your brain has experienced a great trauma. She is unsure how long it will take for your brain to completely heal. Now that you are awake, it is time to help your body relearn things." He smiles as he continues, "We will start with your rehabilitation tomorrow, but today we celebrate that you are awake!"

# THE MISSION
## Chapter Thirteen

I awake the next morning with the memories of last night's celebration on my mind. It brings a smile to my face. I wince. Ouch, that hurt. I think the muscles in my face are sore from all of the smiling.

Last night, Betsy and her parents came to visit. While the parents talked in the hall, Betsy caught me up on everything that had happened over the past months. Summer had ended, and seventh grade had started. They had a fall dance that Betsy went to with our mutual friend Shayla. Betsy told me all about the dance in great detail. It was almost like being there in person.

So much had happened while I had been asleep, making me more ready than ever to start living my life again, but what is that going to look like? My new normal will be much different than it had been.

I smiled the entire time Betsy was here. She told me story after story without need of my verbal response. She is the best! I actually felt like my smile was encouraging her to continue. My heart was so full that it was hard to watch her go when her parents came back into my room to tell her it was time to leave.

Betsy promised she would come back every day that she could, and her parents nodded in agreement. What a great way to end the day. I made a note to myself that today should be celebrated every year. We will call it my Awakening Day.

I felt tired after Betsy left. Mom sat beside me and instructed, "It's time for you to rest. I cannot put into words how thankful I am to have you awake, Grace!" She kissed my forehead.

"I couldn't have said it better," Dad agreed, smiling.

Mom asked me if I would like her to stay with me tonight. I thought a moment before responding, "Yes." She nodded in understanding. She gave my dad a kiss and walked over to the curtained off area of my room. For the first time, I noticed a bed there. As she drew the curtain around to the other side of the bed, I realized this wasn't the first time she had slept here with me.

It looked like she had brought belongings from home to make her time with me more comfortable. I wondered to myself how many nights over the past months she had stayed here with me. It was frustrating not being able to remember. It was like a whole section of my life had disappeared while I was in the darkness. Well, I had a lot of time to make up, as soon as I can get my body moving again.

Mom patted my foot as she passed my bed, taking her small bag to the bathroom to get ready for bed. "I'll be right back," she said. I smiled in response.

I had been trying to move different parts of my body with little success. I would focus on one part and ask it to move. I went from asking to imploring it, demanding it even, but my fingers did little less than twitch. I closed my eyes in frustration. The darkness my eyelids provided was quickly welcomed by my tired body and without another thought, I slipped into a deep sleep.

The sound of the door to my room opens and closes.

"Good morning," I hear my mom say to someone.

The male voice responds, "Good morning! Is she awake yet?"

"Not yet," I hear my mom say.

"Would you like for me to come back?"

"No. Let me wake her." I hear her footsteps come to the side of the bed. "Grace.

Grace, it's time to get up. There is someone I want you to meet."

I will my eyelids to open. His name is Greg, and he is a physical therapist. He is here to help me mobilize my body again. He comes over to my bed and smiles down at me, and I smile back.

"Good morning, Grace." "Good morning," I reply.

"I'm here to help you move your arms and legs." I nod at him. "Do you remember me?"

A blank look runs across my face, and I don't smile. Am I supposed to remember him?

He interrupts my thoughts. "You may not remember me, as the times I've been in to see you, you were sleeping."

Sleeping? He must've come in while I was in the blackness.

"It is so good to finally meet you!" I smile at him. I realized later this would be the last smile he would get from me for weeks to come, for the rest of the time he was with me was filled with pain.

"I'm here," he says, continuing to talk as he works, "to help keep your muscles from atrophying. Do you know what atrophying means?" I don't know what the word means, but he doesn't pause for me to answer and keeps talking as he starts massaging and moving my fingers. The massaging feels good, but when he starts up my arm by rotating my wrist, a shot of pain goes up my arm that causes me to wince.

"Ouch!" I exclaim.

He stops talking for a moment, taking in the look on my face. "I'm here to help you, Grace, but this is going to be painful. The muscles

I was talking about have shortened from not using them. It is my job to help you lengthen and strengthen them again."

I don't smile this time, but I set a firm line to my lips and close my eyes. Without having to say a word, I give him permission to start again.

When he is done, he pats my leg and tells me I have done a good job for today, but that he will be back tomorrow for more. I am so exhausted and sore from him moving every part of my body that I don't and can't imagine what tomorrow is going to be like.

We aren't alone for long before the next therapist enters. This therapist is here to evaluate my speech, or right now my difficulty in being able to speak louder than a whisper. A team of people come that day all with the intention of helping me with my rehabilitation. Each one has a specific role and goal to accomplish.

Over the next couple of weeks, I get to know my team of five therapists. Greg (who I have nicknamed Dr. Pain) has been working on getting me up and moving, and I have made great progress. I am up now, walking a very short distance with a walker. It is a huge win for Dr. Pain and me, and we both know I am getting close to our first goal of getting to go home.

Andrea is my speech therapist. She is helping me to stretch my vocal cords. The way she explained it is that the neural pathways in my brain for speech have been damaged by either the aneurysm or the tumors. We have to work together to create a new path for my brain to direct my tongue and mouth to speak and my throat to swallow.

She, too, is happy with the progress we have made in such a short time. I can speak more now, but my voice is still soft. It hurts to talk too much too often just yet, but Andrea says that is normal. Steve, my hand therapist, and Andrea are working together and coming up with creative ways for me to communicate while my brain is creating new pathways and still healing.

I didn't know until I start working with Steve just how hard it can be to hold a pen or pencil. It's just something else I took for granted that I could so easily do before that now takes momentous effort and focus to do. I roll my eyes again in frustration as I try writing my name. My penmanship looks worse than it had when I was in kindergarten!

Steve in his kind, gentle tone encourages me to try it again. "I promise you won't write like this long. You've made so much progress in such a short time. Just keep trying." I exhale in frustration but am determined to keep going. Keep trying. He looks at the paper in front of me.

"See?" he encourages. "Better already!"

Nancy is my occupational therapist. When I came out of the coma, I was unable to swallow, and I couldn't eat the foods I used to eat. Instead, they had given me a feeding tube with a bag attached that had a beige-colored liquid in it. It is so cool! The tube is connected directly into my stomach. Today is a big day. It is possible I can accomplish another one of my "Go home goals." My go home goals are written on a white board in my room. I had marked off walking yesterday, and today I want to mark off chewing and swallowing.

My go home goals are goals that my body has to be able to do before I can leave the rehab hospital. I can't go home until I am able to chew and swallow.

Nancy comes over with a cup of water. I reach out my hand to take it from her. She holds onto the cup until I nod to her that I have a grasp on it, and she releases it to me. I slowly raise the cup to my lips and take a sip with only a small dribble of water coming out of the side of my mouth. Nancy nods and marks something on the tablet she is holding.

She reaches behind her to the tray she had brought in with her. She takes a spoon and scoops out a spoonful of avocado from a dish. She holds it out to me, making sure I have grasped it before letting go, and I slowly bring the spoon to my mouth. All of the avocado stays in my mouth. I move my jaw up and down, chewing the avocado slightly before swallowing it. I smile. Success!

We continue to go through the items on the tray until she is satisfied.

"Great job, Grace! I will mark this goal off of your list."

"Thank you, Nancy!" I reply softly.

Sara, my nutritionist, stands in the doorway watching our exchange. "Hi, Sara!" I declare. "I can eat!"

"I see that! I guess it is time to change your diet again," she says and points to the bag attached to the feeding tube. "Let's see how you do eating solid foods over the next couple of days, and then we'll get your tube out."

"That would be great!" I exclaim. It had been a difficult last couple of weeks, but it is rewarding to see my body respond and learn new skills. I know I still have a long way to go, but I am hopeful of the possibility of being able to go home in just a few days. I close my eyes, thankful to be alive and thankful at the thought of being able to go home soon.

# GOING HOME
## Chapter Fourteen

This day could not have come soon enough! I can't believe it is finally time to leave! As my mom, dad, and I pack up the room that has been my home for the past months, I again think to myself how thankful I am to be going home.

Over the past month, I have gotten to know some of the other people down the hallway. There are eight rooms total. We are all there for different reasons, but we all have the same desire of getting strong enough to be able to go home. A few never made it home. I saw their personal belongings being moved out of their rooms, preparing the way for the next patient.

It made me sad. Not every person here has family to care about them. They did not have people in their lives who would give them hope and a reason to live. As I continue to take down the items from around the room, my eyes settle on the hope picture.

I tell my mom how I am feeling. I know I am not here by chance. I know I have experienced a miracle. There is no medical reason I should still be alive. I realize as I am standing there listening to my mom talk and taking down my word *hope* on my wall that I can do something. I can leave my hope here.

"Mom," I say, interrupting her mid-sentence. "Can I leave my picture of hope here?

I want to bring hope to others the way these letters and cards brought me hope and encouragement. I don't know quite what that looks like, but if it is okay, can I ask whose room I can leave this in?"

Her eyes well up with tears, and it takes her a couple of seconds before she is able to respond.

"Of course, Grace," she replies.

As if on cue, my nurse walks in the room. I tell her my thoughts and ask if I can pass along my hope picture. She smiles and responds, "I have just the room!"

She leads me down the hallway to one of the newest patient's room. I had heard this person come in but have not yet seen him. On the bed covered in tubes and various other medical equipment is a woman about my mom's age. Sitting by her bed is a man with his head in his hands. My eyes fall on a picture of the man and the woman smiling, looking into each other's eyes as they hold their two small children.

The man looks up toward us. A look of recognition comes across his face when he sees the nurse, but when his gaze meets mine he asks, "Can I help you?"

"Yes," I respond, and I hold out my word picture of hope.

He walks over to me to accept the picture. When his eyes fall on the word, tears start running down his face. I tell him my miracle story and that I want to share with him the same hope I have for his miracle. I look toward the woman. He turns his head toward the bed as well.

"May I?" I ask, gesturing to the picture.

I very tentatively stand from the chair. Mom grasps my elbow in support. I tape the picture of my word *hope* at the foot of his wife's bed.

"Thank you," says the man.

I nod, unable to say anything more as my throat tightens, and the nurse and my mom walk with me out of their room.

I take my mom's hand as the nurse wheels me down the hallway toward the elevator and my dad in the waiting car.

"Mom?"

"Yes, Grace."

"I've found my mission." She turns and looks at me.

"I want to bring hope to people in hopeless situations."

She grabs my hand. "I think that is a beautiful idea, Grace." With that, I stand still, unsteadily but on my own. With one last look at the place that has been my home for the past few months, I say to myself, "I will be back soon to bring more hope